A COWGIRL'S MOVIE STAR

BARRELS AND HEARTS SERIES BOOK 6

EDITH MACKENZIE

Never stop believing

"I don't think we can wait any longer for Frankie, so let's get this meeting started. The twins are running a bit late, too. It took them longer than they anticipated getting home from the rodeo last night. Firstly, Kirk will be arriving in"—Gabi made a show of checking her watch—"exactly three days' time." Excited chatter erupted around the table. Gabi smiled smugly, enjoying the reaction.

A sudden crash of phone and car keys hitting the floorboards silenced the room. "I'm sorry I'm late," Frankie babbled, bending down to scoop up her things, fumbling a few times before being successful. "Um, Gabi, I need to talk to you."

"Sure thing. Let's finish this meeting first and then I'm all yours," Gabi promised, returning to her captive audience. "As I was saying, Kirk will be arriving in three days to begin shadowing Luciano and learning his mannerisms. And the boys are going to show him how to be a convincing bull rider. It'll also give Frankie a chance to start learning lines and scenes with him. Oh, and I found out that Bryce is actually a part owner of the production company. Did anyone know? That man never ceases to amaze me." Gabi looked at Frankie in disbelief. "Do you actually have your hand up to ask me a question?"

Frankie nodded, letting her hand drop. "Um, there might be a slight hitch to your plan." She scrunched her face up anxiously.

"If the boys are being difficult, I'll talk to them. Luciano promised, and Joao will do what I tell him. Kirk has spent the last three months working with a dialect coach to get Luciano's speech patterns right." She turned to Chloe. "Is Travis still onboard to give him time around the bulls?"

"Sure is."

"Um, Gabi," Frankie said, hesitantly shuffling her feet. Gabi noted she still hadn't taken a seat.

"Frankie, are you going to sit down? I'm getting a sore neck looking up at you," Gabi said. Frankie swallowed, finally seating herself, and mumbled something incoherent. "I didn't quite catch that?"

"I'm sitting right next to her and I have no bloody idea what she said either," agreed Deb. "What the bloody heck is wrong with you today? You're acting weirder than usual— and that's really saying something."

Frankie cleared her throat. "I said they're going to have to cast another Frankie."

"What?" exploded Gabi in confusion. "It's a bit late to be backing out now."

"But you're perfect as Frankie," said Chloe.

"It's really like she was born to play it," agreed Deb. "Anyway, we've already organized Chloe to have time off from the ranch and we've even got her a nice new bucket to hold."

Chloe gave Deb a dirty look. "Thanks."

"Don't mention it."

"I'm pregnant." The sound of a pin dropping would have

been deafening in the silence that followed Frankie's quiet statement.

"Are you sure?" Gabi leaned forward, peering at her friend's stomach as if she had x-ray vision.

"Got it confirmed this morning. It's why I was late."

Deb finally gathered her wits. "Oh my gosh. I'm so bloody happy for you." She gathered her friend in a bear hug, thumping her on the back, before remembering her delicate condition and letting her go.

"Edward won't be the baby of the family anymore." Megan rocked on her chair slightly as her son slept soundly in her arms.

"Wait until Sra Ana finds out," Chloe said, her eyes wide at the thought.

"She's going to be eyeball deep in babies and kids soon and loving it," agreed Deb. "Have you told Luciano yet? What did he say?"

Frankie's smile was tender. "He told me that he didn't think he could love me more, but that I'd proven him wrong. He's very excited to be a papai." She glanced hesitantly up at Gabi. "It's okay, isn't it? I mean, it wasn't planned, but…" She left the words hanging.

Gabi smiled joyously at her friend. "Another baby. This movie is nothing compared to that. The producers will just have to find someone else. I wonder who."

"If you'd just listened to me, we would have been here hours ago." Savannah's voice floated angrily through the door. The twins were obviously back home.

"Excuse me for needing to stop. I thought I was going to die."

"You ate too much fried food and you had gas." Savannah curled up her lip in derision as the twins entered the room.

Ash pressed her hand to her side. "It could've been my appendix. I could've ended up in hospital, no thanks to you."

"Oh my gosh, you're such a drama queen. It's like you're always in the darn movies."

Gabi looked across to Frankie, a smug smile on her face. "Perfect."

~

"I DON'T UNDERSTAND why they get to go and meet him, and I'm stuck back here," Ash huffed as she dragged the comb through Shiraz's tail. As the teeth grabbed hold of a gnarled knot, the horse swished his tail in protest. "Sorry, boy." She ceased her agitated grooming to gently tease the strands of hair apart.

"Oh my goodness, Ash, stop with your belly-aching already." Savannah glared at her twin, identical frustration snapping from her eyes. "Get over it."

"And here we go." Chloe sighed from where she was saddling her horse. "You had to go and say it."

Outrage made Ash's mouth drop open. "Get over it? You want me to get over it?" her voice rose several octaves to match her indignation. "I have as much right to be there as any of them." She flipped her hair dramatically, the effect slightly ruined by the smear of dirt on her cheek. "I'll have you remember, I'm Kirk Cooper's co-star, and I should be meeting him today. He's probably expecting it, now that I think about it."

Savannah shook her head slowly, her face a marvel of disbelief at her sister's overblown sense of self-importance. "You can hear how you sound, right?" She picked up her saddle off the rail and placed it on her horse. "You haven't let us forget once since you found out you were replacing Frankie. Has she, Chloe?"

Their blonde friend was suddenly extremely focused on slipping the bridle over her horse's head. "No way am I getting involved in this conversation." She gathered up her reins and gave a little cluck with her tongue. "I'll see you guys in the arena."

"Thanks for the support," Savannah said in disgust, grabbing her own bridle to tack up. "Kirk Cooper probably has no idea who you are and probably isn't the least bit interested." Giving a final check, she gave her sister one last parting shot. "On second thoughts, maybe he's heard about you and asked specifically that you not be there." She ducked as Ash threw the comb at her. "You're going to have to try harder than that. I'll be in the arena, if you ever stop your whining and actually decide to do some work."

It was the injustice of it all that really stuck in Ash's craw. When they'd asked her to do a screen test, she'd dropped everything—including going to a rodeo that she'd arranged to meet up with a very cute cowboy—and she hadn't complained once. Okay, a little, but she'd been discrete when she'd muttered her protests to herself. And what had it gotten her? Left out of it the minute Mr Fancy Pants Movie Star turned up. She grabbed her saddle from the rail, the sudden movement causing Shiraz's head to jerk.

"Come on, boy, I'm the one that's meant to be the drama queen, according to everyone." She reached under the horse's belly for the cinch. "Not that they know anything. I bet they're just jealous. You should have seen Savannah's face when I read the part of the script that had me kissing Kirk." She closed her eyes, practicing the face she would make for the cameras as they panned in for her close-up.

The sound of someone clearing their throat caused her eyes to fly open in horror at the thought of someone seeing her pulling kissing faces. Peering out from underneath her horse she could see a pair of brand new cowboy boots. The leather hadn't even creased yet, looking painfully stiff. A dawning sense of mortification steadily rose through her.

The knowledge that those boots didn't belong to anyone she knew and most likely not anyone from these parts made her swallow.

"Ah, excuse me? Is everything all right down there?" The Californian accent solidified her suspicions. Slowly, straightening inch by inch, she peeked over Shiraz's back, the horror wiping the expression clean off her face.

He looked just like in his movies. The same weathered features, that of a true outdoorsman, so rare in an era of Hollywood pretty boys. Sure, the sunglasses and trucker cap hid his hazel eyes, inherited from his famous father, but there was no mistaking him. Kirk Cooper, in the flesh, was standing in front of her.

She felt like she was in a slow-motion scene from a movie as he removed his sunglasses and hung them from the neck of his shirt. The half smirk on his face had stared out at her from the screen countless time. Her heart pounded as anticipation built.

"Are you Gabriella Cabrera?" he asked.

The words dashed her hopes that he might have recognized her as his co-star. "No, I think you might be in the wrong place. I'm Ash."

His gaze remained blank at the mention of her name, but there was a little gleam of appreciation as he looked at her. "Well, I can't say that I'm upset to meet you. Are all the girls around here so pretty?"

Ash's face grew hot under his admiring look, the pull of his charm putting her under his spell. Giving herself a little shake, she reminded herself that she was a professional actress—or would be, as soon as they started filming. "Gabi's expecting you at Frankie and Luciano's ranch."

"My agent gave me this address."

"Someone got their wires crossed. All I know is that's where everyone is waiting for you. It's not that hard. Go back out the drive, turn left, in two miles you'll see a rusty old tractor in the field. About three miles after that, there's a dirt track. Go down that till you see the dead tree. If you see that tree you know you're on the right track."

Kirk's eyes were beginning to glaze over. "Look, I'm a city boy. Are you able to come with me and show me the way?"

Ash looked from Kirk to Shiraz and to the arena where the other girls rode, oblivious to their famous visitor. Coming to a decision, she nodded. "Let me put my horse away and I'm all yours."

"Just how I like my women." The squinted smirk reappeared, the charm pulling her back in.

Geeze, this man had some major mojo. "I'll meet you at your car." She untied her horse, giving her hips an extra wiggle when she noticed him looking.

"Don't make me wait too long."

THE CAR WAS a luscious gleaming rich red, its lines sleek and lean. It was also very small and low compared to the jacked-up trucks she was used to riding in. Ash settled herself into the passenger seat, feeling uncomfortably close to the ground. She watched, amused as he lowered himself into his seat, his stiff new cowboy boots not giving him enough flexibility to make his descend gracious. A giggle escaped at the spectacle. He shifted in his seat to look at her. "What's so funny?" His wry smile belied the question, making it quite clear he knew exactly why.

"I don't think I've ever seen someone get into a car so awkwardly before." She pursed her lips thoughtfully. "Maybe it's because cowboys usually climb up into their big tough trucks."

Kirk's smile turned wolfish. "Can your big tough trucks

do this?" He floored it, gravel spraying as they shot out of the driveway. Adrenaline coursed through her body—it was electrifying. Ash had never felt so alive. Her smile quickly matched his and he peered closer at her. "You said your name was Ash, didn't you? As in Ash Decker? You're playing Frankie, aren't you?"

Ash smugly pushed herself back in the plush buttery soft leather of the seat. "Well, they wanted a real cowgirl to play her and I'm 100% genuine, the real deal."

When their stares met, his mouth lifted into a wicked smile. "I bet." Ash felt an answering grin creep over her face. This was going to be fun.

She was still buzzing when they pulled up in front of Luciano and Frankie's house. Gabi bustled out to greet Kirk, stopping short when she saw Ash climb up out of the sleek car. She gave Ash a strange look, clearly unsure why she was there and how she'd managed to be there with Kirk. "Hello, Kirk? I'm Gabi. I hope you didn't have any trouble finding the ranch?"

Kirk gave her his best Hollywood smile. Seriously, Ash could understand why he had been cast to play Luciano. They both had the same megawatt smile. "Nothing Ash wasn't able to help me with."

Ash rather enjoyed watching Gabi fight her natural inclination to question him further. It was satisfying to watch the emotions chase themselves across her boss's face. "Well, I'm sure there's a story in that and one I would love to hear sometime. Right now, I'd love to introduce you to Frankie and Luciano."

Ash followed, watching curiously as he interacted with each person he was introduced to. The most fascinating was when he fronted up to Luciano, the mirroring of gestures and body language. Clearly, the man had done his homework.

"Thanks for making sure Kirk arrived safely," Gabi said quietly to Ash, handing her some keys. "You can take my truck back to the ranch and finish your work for the day."

Ash gave her a dark glare, unimpressed that she was being dismissed so easily. Gabi returned her gaze steadily, daring her to argue. Ash was the first to drop her gaze. She might be a hothead, but she wasn't stupid. "I'll see you around, Kirk." She waved, trying to hide her disappointment that she was being forced to leave.

"Ash, once a schedule has been worked out, I want to start going through lines with you," Kirk said.

"Sure, but you'll have to get permission from Gabi first." With a final pointed look at her boss, she waltzed from the room.

The boots bit sharply into his heel, pressing on the raw blister that had formed several days ago. At this rate, his feet were going to break in before the dang boots did. Kirk briefly considered sending an email to his agent to see if he could be sent another pair, this time already broken in, before deciding that was a little too diva even for him. Tender-footed, he did his best to not hobble as he followed Luciano. He closely observed the purposeful swagger of the Brazilian. There was a confidence in each powerful stride that, in a lesser man, would have come across as arrogant, but in this man, it had been earned. Kirk made a mental note to practice adding the extra layer of subtilty to his performance of Luciano when he had a private moment.

Ahead, gathered at the side of a parked truck, four men waited. He could feel the weight of their gaze upon him, gauging his measure. He was pretty certain they didn't really care too much for his celebrity status. For the first time in a long while, he was going to be judged for him.

Luciano shook each of the men's hands, looking each in the eye, the grip firm. Here was a man that was perfectly in control, but at the same time, at ease with himself. "Mitch, Travis, Carlos, Joao, this is Kirk. Kirk, this is Carlos. The blood of a champion bull rider flows through his veins, but he never answered the call. Mitch is no good on a bull, but handy with roping. Travis, he breeds bulls that sound as timid as lambs but will rattle your teeth if you manage to keep them at all. You have already met Joao, an okay bull rider, but he is the bravest of all—he is married to Gabi." The men good-naturedly ribbed Joao for his introduction.

Kirk was a little taken aback that he hadn't been introduced as Kirk Cooper. Ever since he could remember, it had been Kirk Cooper, son of Mason Cooper, legendary Hollywood superstar. He was envious of the easy friendship that bonded the men together, so apparent in their teasing of each other. Growing up in Beverly Hills with the children of other movie stars hadn't been easy. Each had been pitted against the other to try and shine the brightest—but not brighter than their parents.

Trying to harness the confident veneer of his subject, he stepped forward, hand extended. "Pleased to meet you." He gratefully accepted the beer Luciano handed him.

"Today, we will show you what we do best." There was a fierce anticipation glowing in Luciano's eyes, the thrill of the battle about to come. Kirk swallowed down his drink, the excitement steadily beginning to build. He'd always been a thrill seeker, surfing the big waves of Hawaii and rock climbing. But this? This was next level. Who, in the right mind, climbed onto an angry bull for fun? Apparently, these men did. And him, too. Now that he gave it a thought, he wondered if they would let him.

"When he says we, he bloody well means him and, if I wanted to blow smoke up his bum, Joao, too," Mitch said. Kirk was fascinated by the Australian's turn of phrase. There was an almost poetic cadence to it. This visit was proving to be a goldmine for future material.

"I'm mainly here to patch people up, not ride bulls," agreed Carlos.

"Well, it's good to have a doctor in case things go wrong." Kirk was relieved to know there would be a doctor on hand if things went too badly.

"Oh, he's not a bloody doctor." Mitch slapped his leg as he laughed, the idea clearly amusing to him.

"What is he then?"

"I'm a vet," Carlos supplied, once he could be heard over his chuckling friend. "If it makes you feel better, broken bones are broken bones, no matter what animal, man or beast."

Kirk was beginning to wonder what, exactly, he'd signed on for. He knew one thing was for certain—if the studio found out what he was doing, they wouldn't allow it. It was a good thing he was only spectating today. "When do we start?"

Luciano nodded approvingly. "He is eager. Boys, do we let him ride, no? Maybe next time? Travis, who do you have that we could maybe sit him on?"

"Arabesque might be a good one for him to start with." Travis drained the last of his beer and stood.

"Isn't that a dance move?" Kirk wasn't sure he'd heard him right.

"Cheer move, actually." Travis grabbed some strapping from the back of the truck. "I'll go get the bulls into the chute. Let me know when you guys are ready."

It still didn't seem like something normal people did. Mitch looked closely at him. "If you ask me, you have to be a few stubbies short of a six pack to want to ride a bull. Don't let them pull the wool over your eyes. You have the privilege today of watching up close and personal some of the best bull riders of the modern times." He looked guiltily around. "Don't tell Senhor Eduardo I said that, okay, mate?"

Kirk blinked. The words were all English and he understood each individual one, but somehow, he still had no idea what the Australian just said. Carlos laughed at the incomprehension on his face. "I still have no idea what half his sayings mean, and I'm married to an Aussie."

"I am sure my Querida makes things up," agreed Luciano. "Try translating Aussie to American to Portuguese." He picked up a container. "But now, we talk about important things. This is rosin. It is very important."

"You know, I don't think I ever fully appreciated denim before. It really is an amazing fabric." Ash quickly put down the horse's hoof and straightened, spinning around to find Kirk, his characteristic squinty-eyed smirk in place as he eyed her appreciatively. "You didn't need to stop on my account."

"Oh, good you're here, Kirk. Joao told me you're keen to give bull riding a go next time," Gabi said, walking down the stairs from the bunkhouse, the rest of the bosses following her.

"Just don't tell my agent." Kirk winked at her conspiratorially

"Frankie, can you go and get Savannah and Chloe? Tell them that Kirk would like to see what barrel racers do. He wants to understand what you're a champion at." Gabi elbowed her friend, albeit gently. "And since you're busy breeding up some future champs, the girls will have to do."

Gabi's words put a fire in Ash's belly. She was no one's second. Kirk was darn lucky to get to see her do her thing. She was one heck of a barrel racer. Realizing her horse was stepping away from the excessive pressure she was putting behind each stroke, she stopped brushing and threw the brush back into her tack box. She reached for her saddle and then he was there, his hands over hers.

"Let me do that for you." Ash's brows rocketed sky high and she purposely ignored the tingle his touch sent through her. "I know how to saddle a horse. Do you?"

Kirk's mouth twisted in a wry smile. "Never saddled a horse in my life." He rubbed at his jaw. Ash noticed he hadn't shaved for a few days. The stubble gave him a devil-may-care appearance, making him look even hotter than usual.

"Well, stand back and let someone who knows what they're doing get the job done. I'd hate to see you hurt yourself." Ash twitched his hands off and swung the saddle onto the horse's back.

"Ash," warned Gabi. "Remember who you're talking to."

"And he should remember who he's talking to, as well. I've been saddling horses since I was old enough to stand."

"I'm sure he didn't mean anything by it. You know there's nothing wrong with a gentleman offering help," Gabi said.

Kirk spread his hands wide, a darkly amused gleam in his eye. "The lady doesn't need help. Next time, I'll ask instead of stepping on her toes. I'm used to beautiful women who are weak and need looking after. I need to remember beautiful cowgirls are strong and don't need a man for anything."

"Well, I didn't say that. I can think of a few things that a man is handy for." Ash gave him a saucy little smile.

Before long, Savannah and Chloe arrived, saddled their horses, and were ready to ride. A wildness crept over Ash. Each time it was her turn to line up the drums, her blood surged hotly through her veins. She could hear the pounding echo in her ears. Beneath her, the strength and speed of her horse was thrilling. When she found herself waiting for the other girls to have their turns, she would steel glances at

Kirk, curious to see what he made of it all. He whooped and hollered with Gabi and Frankie, and then continued as Deb and Mitch, Senhor Eduardo and Sra Ana joined them. If his eyes seemed to flick her way once in a while, then surely it was just her imagination.

"What did you think?' asked Chloe, circling her horse to cool him down.

"You girls are crazy. I think I understand why Luciano fell in love with a barrel racer. There's a wildness about anyone who wants to ride like that." He looked directly at Ash as he spoke. "It's hot."

Ash felt herself flush under his steady regard. She tossed her head almost in defiance of how he was making her feel. "Well, it's pretty tame at home. If you really want to see what we do, come to a rodeo with us."

Those famous hazel eyes sparkled at her offer. "Challenge accepted."

CHAPTER 3

Country music blared over the loudspeaker, the smell of corndogs and fries strong in the air. Ash's progress was halted as she stopped for a boy crossing in front of her carrying a huge pink cotton candy on a stick. A weight hit her from behind. "Ouch, Savannah, watch out."

"Why on earth are you stopping?" grumbled Savannah. "Don't run into me, Chloe. Ash is causing a traffic jam."

"Just because you won tonight, and it was only by what, 0.02 seconds? Is that even really winning? Doesn't mean you can act all bossy." Ash proceeded now her path was clear. It absolutely ate at her that Savannah had managed to win tonight. She didn't even entertain the notion that some of her angst arose from the fact Kirk had been sitting in the bleachers with the rest of the Affinity Ranch family cheering them on.

"Winners are grinners," Chloe teased from the rear of the group.

"Yeah, what was it Deb tried to get me to say? Rip it up?"

"You bloody ripper." Chloe laughed, looking from one twin to the other.

"Why would I say that? I'm not going to rip up my check." Savannah looked at her sister, bafflement making her face scrunch up.

"That would just be silly," agreed Ash. Honestly, Aussies were just plain strange sometimes. "Why would we compete if we were just going to tear it up? We do it for the prize money."

"And bragging rights. It just means that you did very well." Chloe waved at Teeny where she stood beside Travis and the rest of their friends. "If you're worried about what Kirk thinks, just tell him you won, and the announcer got confused when he announced it." She gave Ash a saucy wink and, apparently happy to leave her stewing on the idea, waltzed off to give her husband a kiss.

"Don't even think about it," warned Savannah. "I won fair and square."

"Why are you always so mean to me?"

"How am I being mean to you? I won, you lost. Like you would do if the roles were reversed."

It was hard to argue with that. Shrugging her shoulders, she straightened her hat and headed over, following in Chloe's footsteps. Kirk stood in the midst of the guys. Ash couldn't quite put her finger on it, but somehow, it was like he was blending in, becoming one of them. "Bad luck," he greeted her.

"Don't even get her started," Savannah grumbled from behind. "She hasn't stopped whining about it the entire way over."

"All I'm saying is there was nothing in it." Ash inspected her nails closely.

"There was 0.02 seconds in it."

"Is that even actually a measurement of time?"

Savannah looked at her in open-mouthed amazement.

"Of course it is. Oh my gosh, Ash, it's the whole reason they have timekeepers."

"Whatever. Still think they made a mistake." Ash, deciding that all she was achieving was making herself look like a sore loser, smiled graciously at her sister. "If I was going to draw with someone for first place, I'm glad it's you."

"We didn't draw. I won." Savannah ground out.

"I don't think I can do this." Frankie turned and buried her face into her husband's chest.

Deb looked at her sympathetically. "I feel your pain. It helps when you get a break from their arguing when they're out on the road."

"You don't understand," sobbed Frankie. "I'm having twins."

In the midst of the noisy crowded rodeo grounds, it was suddenly as if they were in an oasis of stunned silence. "Two new grandbabies." Sra Ana looked up at Senhor Edwardo, stunned wonderment in her voice. "We're having two new grandbabies."

Joao cuffed Luciano on the shoulder. "I should have known you would not be happy doing it like a normal person. Congratulations, my friend."

Luciano took the other Brazilian's hand in a firm grasp. "Thank you, it will be your time soon. We will have little bull riders and barrel racers running rings around us."

Ash thought Joao looked sad at Luciano's words, the expression at odds with the sentiments of the words spoken to him. Confused, she looked to Gabi and saw a similar sadness swimming in the depths of her dark eyes.

"This calls for a celebration or a commiseration, depending on your point of view. I, for one, can't wait to meet the little ankle-biters." Mitch raised his beer. "And I appear to be empty. Shall we mosey on over to the bar and continue?"

Music spilled out into the night air as the group relocated. Ash's foot began to tap, her body gently swaying in time with the beat. "Dance with me?" Kirk held his hand out, a dark inviting light in his gaze, that darn hot-as-all-heck half smirk on his lips.

"Do you think you can keep up?" she sassed, signaling for him to follow, hips swishing as she sashayed out onto the dance floor.

"I have no idea, but I want to find out."

Ash threw her head back and laughed exuberantly as he pulled her into his strong arms, the music pulsing through her. There was a deliciousness in being held by him as they moved together. A wildness made her blood burn hot. All she wanted was to be close enough for his musky scent to make her head swim with a heady intoxication. "I don't know if I've ever met someone quite like you."

Those smoldering eyes crinkled. "A movie star? You don't seem very impressed that I'm famous."

She gave an indelicate unladylike snort. "Oh, I'm very impressed. The thing is, I won't change how I act just because of who you are." She shrugged, still secure in his arms. "Why on earth would I? I'm awesome how I am, no matter who you are."

Kirk laughed, his teeth flashing pearly white. "I'm beginning to notice how awesome you are."

"Is that what you're doing? Don't take too long to fully appreciate it, I might decide to take my awesomeness elsewhere."

His arms tightened around her, his expression intent on her face. "I don't think you're going anywhere."

A thrill shot through her at the possessiveness of his words. She saw her own recklessness reflected back at her.

"Well, hang on tight, cowboy. It's gonna be one heck of a ride."

~

"Let's start at the beginning," Kirk instructed, his tone professional as he pointed at the script that lay in Ash's lap.

She bit her lip to stop herself from laughing at the image of Mr Kirk, the teacher. She followed his gesture and picked up the bound paper from her lap. It was large with a brass stud at the top and bottom holding the single-sided printed pages together.

"Every script is made up of the same components. Firstly, each page is roughly the equivalent of one minute of screen time, but that's obviously dependent on how they edit it. The dialogue is pretty self-explanatory. On the left is which character is speaking. The action, also called screen direction, is written in present tense. Now, at the start of each scene is the slug line. It contains three pieces of information. Whether the scene is inside or exterior, the notation for inside will be INT for interior, and EXT for exterior. Then, it's the location and the time of day the scene is to be set in. And that's your standard script."

Ash pushed down the nauseous, fluttery feeling in her belly, briefly considering that she might have gotten herself in over her head as she bit down on her fingernail. "Okay, that sounds fairly easy to remember." She hoped she sounded convincing. "So, what's next?"

"You learn your lines, and then you learn them some more, and then, when you think you know them by heart, you learn them some more."

"How do you get into character?" She'd seen Kirk writing notes on his phone and repeating a gesture that he had just seen Luciano do. She'd never fully appreciated just how involved it all was.

He rubbed his jaw slowly with his thumb. Ash found her eyes riveted to the rhythmic gesture. "Every actor has a different method. I worked with a dialogue coach before I came here—I really wanted to get the accent right. It helped, but Luciano has lived in America for a while now, so some of his words or how he says something is a hybrid between the two. You will find Frankie is the same. She obviously has an Australian accent, but now she rolls her *r* a bit like a Texan."

"I'm pretty good at mimicking people. All I think about for Frankie is one of their crazy Aussie sayings and then BAM! I'm right there." Ash never thought the skill that had made her popular in high school—well one of them—would prove to come in handy. Take that, Mr Groverstein, it's proven more useful than your dumb algebra.

"Do you want to start practicing some lines?' He settled down on the grass beside her. It had been his suggestion to find somewhere they wouldn't be disturbed to hold their practice sessions. She hadn't even known this shady little spot that overlooked Frankie and Luciano's ranch even existed.

Ash gripped her script tightly, turning to the first page. "Ready when you are." If she thought it was a matter of saying some words between them to begin remembering the lines, she was sadly mistaken. After about an hour of practice she was ready to throw the darn script into the bushes.

"I know it's a lot to commit to memory, but you need to learn it how you are going to say it. Step into Frankie's shoes, how is she feeling when she says it? Why is she saying it to Luciano?"

Ash rubbed at her eye in frustration. "I don't know if I can do this. I mean, it seemed like a good idea at the time, but now... I think they've made a mistake casting me as Frankie. What happens if I ruin this? What happens if I make lots of mistakes when we start filming? I don't even know what happens on a set." She sucked in a shuddering breath, nausea rising in her throat at embarrassing herself in front of all the Hollywood people.

Seeking her hand with his own, he tangled their fingers together. "I promise I'll take care of you. I won't let you make too many mistakes." He grinned at her. "Well, I'll try. You probably won't listen to me."

"Promises, promises. You're probably right, I probably won't listen. You'll just have to make me." She swore she could feel sparks flying from where their hands were still entwined. "So, when you're not learning lines and how to become someone else, what do you do for fun?"

"Hit the strip, surf, fish, ride dirt bikes, rock climb. I hang out with my buddies a lot when I'm home. I love the ocean. I think it's from when my dad filmed a series of movies in Hawaii. It was one of the best times of my life. I used to spend all day at the beach."

"I like fishing and, believe it or not, I can ride dirt bikes and I'm not half bad." Ash blew on her fingers modestly. "I think Dad really wanted a son."

He looked at her, surprise and admiration a wonderful mix on his face. He gave a little laugh. "Actually, I'm not surprised. I think, when I'm around you, I'm learning to throw out everything I know or expect from women. You are nothing like the women I know."

"I'll take that as a compliment."

"You should. I hope you never become like them." Kirk stared off into the distance.

Ash felt like he had gone somewhere else in his mind. "What was it like growing up as Mason Cooper's son?"

"You know, that's the first time you've ever called me his son." He squinted at her, the look uncanny in its resemblance of his famous father. "I liked that about you." Kirk pulled himself up till he was reclining on one elbow. "What was it like being Dad's son?" He shrugged. "Dad was away a lot, working on movie sets. Sometimes, we were allowed to come with him and that was really cool. When he was away, my mom would read about him and his female co-stars, and then she'd drink for days. But I did have some nice nannies. When Dad hired them, they were young, blonde, and perky. When I was little, I thought they were fun because they would play games with me and then, when I got older, well, my friends would give me high fives when whichever nanny I had at the time picked me up from school. When Mom hired them, they were fat, old and grumpy. Then Dad would breeze back in from whatever country he had filmed his latest movie in, and then I would get lots of gifts and Mom would put on her most beautiful dresses and have her hair and makeup done. She would be so happy as they left for parties."

Ash felt sad for the younger Kirk. She wished she could gather that little boy up in her arms and shower him with love. "That doesn't sound so great."

"It wasn't all bad. I mean, my first car was a corvette and I threw some killer parties in high school."

She knew he wouldn't appreciate her pity, but that didn't stop her from allowing her sympathy to show. "I don't know if I'd like to have been Mason Cooper's son."

Once again, his hazel eyes drifted to the horizon, the lush ranch vista spilling out before him. "I don't recommend it."

CHAPTER 4

The man was short, almost as wide as he was tall. A resemblance to a little bustling beaver was the first thought that rather unkindly sprung to Ash's mind when he waddled into the barn with Gabi and Frankie.

"Would we have access to all of this for shooting the training scenes if we required?" His voice was nasally and high-pitched. Ash found herself watching agog, fascinated at what had just landed in their midst. A quick sideways glance proved the sight was just as irresistible to Savannah beside her and Deb further down the barn.

"Obviously, we're a working ranch, but we can work around a schedule as required." Gabi, spying Ash, smoothly guided her guest in her direction. "Walter, this is Ash Decker — she's playing Frankie—and her sister, Savannah. Girls, this is Walter Benson, he's the film's location manager."

Sharp beady eyes scanned her from head to toe, and then quickly assessed Savannah. "Why had no one mentioned she's an identical twin?"

Gabi seemed unsure why it seemed such a pertinent piece of information. "No one asked."

"This will be a real asset to filming." He tapped on his earpiece and walked away, muttering as he talked to someone on the line.

Frankie looked wide eyed between the waddling back of the departing man and the others. "What just happened?" She'd taken the words straight out of Ash's mouth. Why was he so interested in Savannah? Ash was the one starring with Kirk.

"Somehow, I think you might be more involved with the film than anyone had anticipated," Gabi remarked. She shuffled from foot to foot, as if wondering if she should follow after Walter or discreetly remain behind.

"No!" both Ash and Savannah exclaimed at the same time. They turned to each other, irate at the others comment.

"What do you mean 'no'?" huffed Ash, hands firmly on her hips as she squared up to her sister. "Do you think you're too good to be involved?"

"I know I'd be terrible at being involved. I'm no Hollywood type. But what do *you* mean 'no'? Do you think I'm not good enough, that you're the only one?" Anger snapped from emerald eyes as Savannah mirrored her twin.

"Geeze, put a sock in it," Deb groaned.

"What?" The twins asked confused.

"Peace. Deb's just saying let's have a little peace and quiet," Frankie said. "I think I'd be lucky to have either or both of you girls being part of a movie about me and Luciano." Gabi nodded in agreement, obviously happy to let Frankie handle this one. "But we don't know exactly what he meant, so let's not go getting ahead of ourselves."

"Ash, if you start acting like a diva to me, it's not going to end well," Savannah warned, grabbing a halter and heading out to catch a horse.

"Hey, who are you calling a diva?" Ash called after her.

"Not that I'm saying I would personally call you one, but

if the shoe fits, strap that sucker on and wear it." Deb smiled sweetly as she cruised past, pushing a wheelbarrow.

Ash was struck by the injustice of it all. If anything, she was the low-maintenance twin. "Do you guys think I'm a diva?" she asked Frankie and Gabi.

"I really should go see where Walter has ended up." Gabi briskly walked off to find the misplaced man.

"Frankie?" Ash pleaded. Surely Frankie could be relied on to agree with her.

Frankie looked down at her watch, a harried expression as she nibbled her bottom lip. "Wow, is that the time? Luc will be wondering what happened to me. And then I promised Megan I would drop in and see her." Her pace was only slightly slower than Gabi's had been moments earlier.

"Nice one, guys, real nice. I'll remember this when you want an autograph."

THE BREEZE WAS GENTLE, the horses tried hard, and the sun shone. It was difficult to stay mad for too long when it was a day like this. A silver truck pulled in, one she hadn't seen before, and she assumed it had been hired by someone to drive Walter around in. She paused a moment to admire the toughness of the rig, the shiny rims and polished alloy. The dark tinted window wound down and Kirk gave her his best devil-may-care smirk.

"Enjoying the view?"

"It's a hot looking truck. It's enough to turn a girl's head." Ash fanned herself. "What happened to your fancy sports car?"

"It's safe and sound, don't you fear. It's ... well, this one feels like a better fit. Are you finished for the day?"

She sniffed at the memory of the treatment she'd received

from her friends that morning. "I'm more than ready to call it a day. Why? What did you have in mind?"

That sexy boyish smile did funny things to her stomach. "Look in the back."

Curious, she had to stand on her tiptoes to peer in. Her questing eyes widened when she sighted the cooler and fishing rods. "Why didn't you lead with that?" She climbed in the truck, the aroma of the new car smell delighting her senses. "Now, I just so happen to know about a super-secret spot a few miles down the road."

Kirk gunned the engine and the big truck roared to life, leaving a shower of gravel in their wake.

ASH SAT on the creek bank. It felt heavenly to have her boots off and jeans rolled up, the cool water delicious as it massaged her feet. She listened to the water trickling along as she watched a lone dragonfly skim across the surface of the creek, sending little ripples whenever it delicately touched the surface. A fishing rod was held loosely in her hand. As with her other free hand, she brought a beer to her lips. She sighed contentedly, for a moment at perfect peace with the world. "Now this is living."

"It feels like a lifetime ago since I was in LA. I can't say I'm exactly missing it." He took a sip from his beer. "Not when I'm drinking a brew with a beautiful woman and holding my rod." Ash spluttered at his words, causing Kirk to grin mischievously at her. "I love that I can be me around you. I can let down my guard and it doesn't matter. It's like you see me as Kirk, not Kirk Cooper the movie star, not Mason Cooper's son. Just Kirk."

"Of course I want Kirk." Ash blushed, realizing she might have committed a little too readily. "Kirk Cooper the movie star doesn't exist, he's just a fantasy. A very hot fantasy, but not real. Not someone I can touch."

They remained still as they held each other's gaze. "Does this mean you've thought about touching me?" he asked, his eyes intent.

Ash tucked a wayward strand of hair behind her ear, breaking the contact. "I might have thought about kissing you once or twice."

He smiled smugly at her, his eyes heavy lidded. "Why haven't you?"

She fiddled with her fishing rod, feeling like she was drowning in the intensity of the emotions he stirred within her. Giving up, she put it on the ground beside her and shifted until she faced him fully, leaving her vulnerable to his seeking gaze. "Well, down here, a lady waits for the gentleman to do the kissing first."

Warm fingers brushed over her face gently. "That would never work in LA. The girls are a little more aggressive there."

"Well, you're not in LA now," she said tartly, uncomfortable that he might compare her to the girls back there and find her lacking.

His hand was insistent as he forced her chin upwards so that he was the only thing reflected in her eyes. "You have no idea how thankful I am that I'm not in LA right now." His lips hovered inches from hers until she felt like she would explode if he made her wait a second longer. Before she could get any words out, he covered her mouth with his, kissing her deeply. Closing her eyes to savor the sensation of his lips on hers, Ash was thankful he wasn't in LA either.

CHAPTER 5

The grape jelly oozed from the sandwich as Ash bit into it, the flavor mixing with the peanut butter as she chewed. Kirk sat across from her, a far different man than the one that had turned up in his fancy sports car pretending to be a cowboy. This Kirk was still an actor—the script he was reading lines from was mute evidence of that—but now, he seemed real. The tightness around his eyes that Ash hadn't even noticed until they were one day gone had made her realize how uptight and stressed he was when they'd first met. He'd unhappily been cast in a role he'd never auditioned for and now, out here with her, he'd thrown off the shackles of being Mason Cooper's son.

He looked up and caught her staring at him. "What?" He rubbed at his mouth as if to locate the smear of food that made her look at him so. "Maybe I put too much jelly on when I made the sandwiches."

He would never know how much it meant to her each time he turned up with lunch to share with her—a lunch that, no matter how humble, he had made for her. Ash didn't think she had ever eaten anything as delicious as the sandwich dripping its filling all over her hand. "Is there even such a thing as too much?" To prove her point she finished off the last of it and licked her fingers clean.

He watched, transfixed, as she placed each finger in her mouth, his hot-as-all-heck half smile making his eyes hooded and mysterious. "I've never been so envious of fingers before."

Ash felt her face burn furiously at the meaning of his words. "Are there any lines you want to go over, or should we continue after I finish work?"

He looked at her, sighing regretfully as he brushed his hands clean. "I think you've memorized all your lines. Maybe the kissing scenes could do with a little extra work, but only because I'm a professional."

"It's funny, three months ago I didn't know you and filming seemed like it was ages away, and now it's hard to imagine not seeing you each day and, when I think about how close we are to starting filming, I feel sick." Ash looked away, scared that he would see how close she was to terror at the thought of not only the filming starting, but it ending and never seeing him again.

"I promised I would look after you on set, but after practicing lines with you all this time, I think you'll be fine." He stood up and then helped Ash to her feet as well. "I'll see you tonight." She leaned into him as he kissed her, the feel of his hard body against her reassuringly real. Ash watched him fold up the picnic blanket before waving him goodbye.

She should have known that her lunchtime rendezvous would not have escaped the notice of the girls. Ash had barely stepped back inside the barn before it started.

"I think you guys are the sweetest things I've ever seen." Chloe was doe eyed as she clutched her hands to her heart.

"It's very romantic," agreed Frankie.

Deb rolled her eyes. "Like it was ever going to end any other bloody way."

Chloe furrowed her brow, confused by Deb's statement. "What do you mean?"

Megan bounced Edward on her knee where she sat on the bunkhouse steps. "I think I know what Deb's on about."

"You do?" Ash asked, unable to help herself. If they were going to talk about her, she sure as heck was going to be part of the conversation. "Do you know what everyone's going on about?" she asked Savannah.

Savannah shrugged. "No idea, but that's a lot of the time when Deb's talking."

"Australian is the same as the Queen's English, I'll have you bloody know. You're acting like I'm trying to pull the wool over your eyes." Deb, offended, glared at the twins.

Ash couldn't resist. "See, there she goes again. I have no idea what she just said to me."

Deb rolled her eyes heavenward. "Well, you're playing Frankie, and Kirk's playing Luciano, and together, you're both playing Frankie and Luciano falling in love."

Chloe's eyes went wide at the poetic image. She clutched her hands together. "Isn't that just the most romantic thing?"

Ash wasn't quite so enamored by Deb's observations. She looked flatly at her. "I'd like to think it's Kirk and Ash that're falling in—" She abruptly stopped herself, a sinking sensation settling in her stomach at the realization that it didn't matter. She had already revealed too much, and there was no way her friends were going to miss her slip up. "Well, that it's us. Not us playing Frankie and Luciano," she finished lamely.

Savannah stared at her like she had suddenly grown a second head. "Were you just about to say fall in love?"

"No."

"You totally were." Savannah gaped at her. "Have you guys actually said it?"

"Shut up, Savannah. I've got work to do." Ash stormed out of the barn.

"Hey, we're not done talking to you." Deb laughed.

"Too late, I'm gone," Ash yelled as she beat a hasty retreat out into the relative safety of the field.

CHAPTER 6

The line of trucks, trailers, and everything in between snaked through the gate, a convoy of proportions that Ash hadn't been expecting for a film set. The early arrivals were already being ushered into place for all the world looking like they were preparing to establish a small village.

"I'm glad we paused building the new facilities while this was going on. I don't know where we would have fit everyone otherwise," Frankie said, shading her eyes as she watched the unfolding spectacle before her.

"I heard when I was in the feed store the other day that all accommodation within twenty miles of here has been booked out," Joao said.

Ash's head swam at the commotion. She swallowed, her mouth suddenly feeling like it had too much saliva. Her legs twitched as she fought against the need to flee. Savannah shook her head in stunned amazement. "I knew a movie set would have a few people working on it, but this is ... I have no words."

"That'll be a bloody first." Deb snorted. The snarky reply

Ash was about to retort on behalf of her sister died on her lips when she saw Kirk and Gabi making their way to the porch where everyone had gathered to watch. A thin, incredibly fashionably attired woman was with them. She walked a little too close to Kirk for Ash's liking.

Kirk bounded up the steps and gave Ash a kiss, somewhat mollifying the surge of jealousy she felt toward the scrawny stranger. It didn't escape her notice that the woman didn't look pleased at his action. "Ash, this is my agent, Desiree. Desiree, this is Ash Decker."

Desiree gave Ash a polite smile—one that didn't disguise the hardness around her mouth or the coldness in her eyes. "Ah, the unknown replacement to play Frankie. I wasn't aware you had become a method actor, Kirk." Ash wondered if it was considered unprofessional to slap an agent on the first day on set.

"I'm not. Ash and I are together." The words were so simple, so powerful once spoken.

Those cold eyes swept Ash and obviously found her wanting and not worth further consideration. "Is it always this dusty? I haven't seen it like this since we did that film in Namibia. My Lord, we were so eager to get back to LA. I bet you can't wait to return to civilization after this one, too."

Kirk's hand was warm where it rested on Ash's shoulder easily, his arm around her. "It's hardly the wilds of Africa," he protested. "There's something about this place. It gets under your skin. I think it's going to be hard to leave." Ash's mouth went dry, her heart plummeting. She'd always known that Kirk would have to return to his normal life. Well, as normal as it gets for a movie star. A life that didn't include her. "Maybe I'll have to take some of it with me." He looked at her, his eyes warm with his feelings for her and, just like that, her despair was swept away. A worry for another day.

"Ash, welcome. I'd like to introduce you to the cast." Spence Wittnall, the director, ushered her into the room when he saw her standing hesitantly on the threshold. "I understand you and Kirk are already familiar with each other."

"That's what I heard, too," a large dark-haired man said, guffawing at his joke. "I can't wait to get familiar with her myself." Ash blushed under the attention and innuendo. She tried not to scuttle too quickly to the seat that had been kept free beside Kirk.

"Funny thing, the longer I spend here, the more I find myself agreeing with the cowboy code," Kirk began conversationally. "And if you ever say anything like that about Ash again, I'll break your darn face." There was a threat of violence on his face that Ash had never seen before. She straightened her spine and raised her chin defiantly. She had nothing to be ashamed of and dang if she was going to let them make her feel like she did.

Spence went around the table making introductions. It was one of the most bizarre experiences of her life—meeting people that bore a fleeting resemblance to her friends. Kirk whispered that it would blow her mind to see them once they were in full makeup and wardrobe. Spence cleared his throat to gain their attention. Ash felt like a child that had been caught gossiping in class by the teacher.

"Speaking of which, Ash, I believe they are waiting for you in wardrobe."

And just like that, she was dismissed and went in search of her next meeting. Savannah appeared out of one of the side lanes that had been left for ease of access around the labyrinth of trailers. "How did it go?"

"It was so weird. The lady they cast as Deb, she did a quick impression and oh my gosh, I can't wait for Deb to hear herself." Ash looked at her twin curiously. "Where are you off to?"

"I've been ordered to wardrobe."

"Me too, and I think we're there." Ash opened the door and entered a hive of activity.

Every square space was covered or filled or had someone working. Racks upon racks of clothing stood in neat rows, little cards with the character's name above and tags swinging off them. Shoes were lined up neatly below. In the corners, between shelves of accessories, were dress mannequins. On other walls were giant calendars, notes scribbled all over them. A middle-aged woman sat at one of the desks, a giant notepad in front of her and a jar of markers. Glasses hung from a chain around her neck. "Ah, Ash and Savannah Decker, I assume, since I can't rightly tell the two of you apart." She stood and extended her hand. "I'm Martha, the wardrobe manager."

Ash shook her hand. "I'm Ash, but I'm confused about why Savannah is here."

"She needs to be measured in case the two of you aren't the same size."

"I'm not fatter than her," huffed Savannah. "But why would it matter anyway?"

"Because you're her double and fill in." Martha smiled at the perplexed expressions of the twins. "When Ash isn't required to be on the set to deliver lines—it might be a shot that only shows the back of her head, for example—then you will be filling in for her. In your case, you will be doing a lot more because, well, you're identical. No one will be able to tell the difference. That will free Ash up to prepare for upcoming scenes."

"Back up the apple cart. I never agreed to that." Savannah sounded panicked.

"You'll have to take it up with your agent. All I know is

today, I am measuring you. I also need to make sure the wigs fit you."

"What?" both girls exclaimed.

"The wigs?" Martha questioned, unsure what the twins were seeking clarification on.

"What do you mean wigs?' Ash demanded, her hand flying to her own luscious locks.

"You don't need to worry about them, only Savannah." Ash looked smugly at Martha's words, enjoying her twin's appalled expression. "Obviously, you will be bleached blonde."

"What?" Ash now was uncomfortably aware that hers and Savannah's roles of only moments earlier had been reversed. A quick glance confirmed her suspicion. "What do you mean bleached? I've always been auburn."

"You have met Frankie?" Martha asked. "I was under the impression that you worked for her or something."

"Yeah, we both do," Savannah said, her furrowed brows lifting as enlightenment dawned across her face and she began to giggle. "Oh, this is going to be too funny."

Martha looked from the chuckling twin to the stony-faced one. "How did you think you were going to play a blonde Frankie and not be blonde?"

Ash's hand flew protectively to her hair. "But I've never dyed my hair in my entire life," she protested.

Martha's expression was entirely unsympathetic. "There's a first time for everything. I suggest, next time, you read the contract your agent sends you a little more carefully."

"Do we even have an agent?" Savannah asked Ash.

"I'm not sure," whispered Ash. "If you laugh at me being blonde, I swear I will bleach your hair during the night."

"You'd never." Savannah stared at her aghast.

"Try me."

CHAPTER 7

At the beginning, the changes were subtle and so few it was easy to dismiss them, but once Ash notice them, they ate away at her. Ever since the Hollywood crew had arrived, Kirk had changed. Sure, he was still attentive and caring, but his eyes were more guarded now, his mannerism more that of Kirk Cooper rather than Kirk, the man who had stolen her heart. It didn't help that Desiree was always around, pulling him aside to discuss new scripts or photoshoots once the film was wrapped.

"Do you notice anything different about Kirk?" she asked Savannah as she walked through the trailer village. "He's not the same, is he?"

Savannah cocked her head, reminding Ash of a little bird peering down at her from a branch. "What do you mean?"

"It's like there are all these parts of him that he never shared with me before. Where did Kirk go? Sometimes I'm not sure who is holding me—Kirk, or Kirk Cooper, movie star. I wonder if I'm enough for him now." Ash felt incredibly sad as she spoke. She hadn't realized before she'd uttered the words just how true they were and how insignificant it made her feel.

"Well, sure, he's different now." Savannah shrugged as she scanned about her, trying to find her bearings. "He's a movie star. He couldn't act just like us anymore, could he?"

"I guess not. But you don't know him the way I do." She kicked at a tuff of grass in her way. "Or, at least, the way I thought I knew him."

"Honestly, I think you're overthinking it. From what I can see, he's still really into you. Anyway, I have to get to this fitting since you're apparently too important to waste your time on insignificant things like this now."

Ash looked her sister up and down. "Are you sure you haven't gained a few pounds? I don't want you making me look chubby on screen."

"Our measurements are exactly the same. That's how I got roped into these darn fittings for you. So, Ash, if you think I look chubby, go take a long hard look in the mirror." With a flick of her hair, Savannah waltzed off, heading to wardrobe, leaving her sister staring at her departing back and fuming.

SAVANNAH WAS STILL CONGRATULATING herself on her sharp retort to her sister when she stepped into the wardrobe trailer. Fancy Ash trying to say she was getting chubby.

"I hope that pretty smile is for me."

Her head jerked at the sound of the familiar male voice. "Bryce! What on earth are you doing here?" She quickly stepped into his welcoming embrace, enjoying the smell of his expensive aftershave.

"I'm providing a lot of the clothes for Frankie and Luciano's characters. We want it to be authentic, after all."

Martha placed her spectacles on her face and brought out the massive book that took pride of place on her worktable. "These are some of the looks I was thinking for Frankie."

Bryce peered down, his brows pulled together thoughtfully, and then looked up at Savannah. For a moment, she wasn't sure if he saw her or Frankie. "I think you'll find the clothes I've brought will give you the style you want. I've also got a few I think you might be interested in trying. They'd look good on screen."

Martha pushed her glasses back from where they had slipped perilously close to sliding off the tip of her nose. "We've got the double today. If it was the actress, I would hesitate, but let's try everything on and decide."

"Way to make a girl feel special," Savannah muttered.

The wardrobe manager gave a little humph, completely unapologetic. If anything, the noise was to say Savannah was making a big deal out of nothing. Bryce removed his hat and held it lightly to his chest. "I do apologize for any offense mine and Martha's words might have caused. Can you find it in your heart to forgive me?"

"Don't look at me like that." Savannah wagged her finger sternly at him.

"Like what?"

"Like a puppy dog that has chewed up my slipper and, now that the damage is done, is giving me their cutest look so they can't get a telling off." Truth be told, Savannah was happy to see him smiling, even if she thought his eyes still looked a little sad. She briefly wondered what could have caused the shadows she always saw there.

"Then, you forgive me? Or do I need to wag my tail a little first?" He gave an exaggerated wiggle of his hips, causing Savannah to giggle and Martha to frown disapprovingly.

"For now."

"Good, because ya'll going to love the clothes I've brought with me today."

"Did you pick them? Anyway, I was never really mad at you, it's just I never really wanted to do anything on this film. It was Ash's gig, and now I'm left to do all the things that she doesn't want to do or is too important for." Savannah began taking her boots off at Martha's direction.

"Ash is the one missing out. You get to spend the day with a charming, handsome man and try on clothes." Bryce's smiling face was disarming. There was something about being around him that made Savannah feel good.

"When is this man arriving?" She pretended to look around expectantly. The dour Martha laughed as she rolled over a railing of clothing and began to select items from it.

Bryce held his hand to his heart. "Ouch. I declare you have wounded me to my core. Only the kiss of a pretty maiden will make it better."

"Well, this pretty maiden needs to try these clothes on," Martha said, thrusting some garments into Savannah's unprepared hands. Quickly she clutched at the bundle, attempting to not drop anything. With an exaggerated haughty sniff, Savannah high-tailed it to the changing room.

What followed was an endless cycle of being handed a complete outfit and changing into it before stepping out for the others to see. Martha would bustle over, adding, changing, and often removing accessories till she was satisfied with the look. She would also pin and take notes of what needed to be altered for a better fit. Bryce made himself comfortable in Martha's chair, a move that didn't go unnoticed by the wardrobe manager.

Savannah always knew from Bryce's face what he thought of each outfit. It was to be expected, since it was his clothing line that she was parading before him. Finally, after a long day of standing, turning and being pinned, muttering to herself, she tried on the last outfit. This one fit snuggly as it settled over her hips. The white lace made her feel deliciously womanly. With one final shimmy to make sure the fabric was where it ought to be, she pulled open the curtain and stepped out.

The effect on Bryce was satisfying to say the least. His jaw gaped open, eyes wide, before they roamed over her body, inspecting every inch. Savannah felt strangely vulnerable under his intense gaze and folded her arms over her chest. Martha quickly slapped them away and back to hanging at her side as she added a belt and necklace. She handed her a pair of boots to put on before she stepped back to admire her handiwork.

"Well?"

"I had Luciano describe what Frankie wore the night they met. This is what I came up with," Bryce said. "It's no wonder he fell in love with her on the spot."

"It looks all right, then?" Savannah asked, the look in his eyes telling her more than any mirror could. Still, the female vanity in her demanded the satisfaction of seeing what had caused such a visible reaction in Bryce.

"Look for yourself." Martha dragged over a mirror for her to look into.

She already knew that the white lace dress fitted her like a glove in all the right places. Before flaring from the point of her hips, her waist was cinched in with a turquoise belt. The neckline was cut to give the merest suggestion of cleavage, a turquoise squash blossom necklace contrasting with her tan. Her reflected eyes glowed back at her, their bright emerald green somehow brighter.

"Wow." Suddenly, she felt insanely jealous that Ash would get to wear this outfit and, after she took it off today, she never would again.

"Wow, indeed," Bryce agreed.

"Well, I think we're all in agreement that this works for the Luciano and Frankie meeting scene." Martha reached for her camera. "Move away from the mirror so I can take a picture, and then I'd say we're done for today."

CHAPTER 8

The foundation was cool against Ash's skin as the makeup artist applied it, following the contours of her face. She scratched at the back of her hand, the nerves making her itchy. Or maybe it was her brain trying to distract her from the urge to vomit. Sitting still and trying to appear calm was pure torture. To make matters worse, Savannah was sitting beside her happily browsing her phone, not a care in the world. "Bet you won't be so calm when it's your turn," Ash muttered under her breath, conveniently forgetting that she had gleefully seized the opportunity that now felt like a noose around her neck.

"Close your eyes, please," the makeup artist instructed.

Ash felt like she was in danger of exploding, her thoughts whirling as fast as her stomach churned. "I don't know why you even bothered being here, Savannah, if all you were going to do was sit on your phone. The whole reason I asked if you wanted to come with me was so I had someone to talk to, not so I could watch you on your stupid phone. It's so typical of you." She swallowed down her fear, the horrible sensation that she was about to make an epic idiot out of herself. "What if I've made a big mistake? I'm a barrel racer, for goodness sake, not an actress. Who am I kidding? I'm never going to pull this off. I'm so scared, Savannah." She glanced over at her sister, still glued to her phone. "Are you even listening?"

Without looking up, Savannah nodded. "Sure am."

"What did I say?" Ash obediently looked up to have her mascara applied.

"Boo hoo, I'm scared, everyone's going to laugh at me because I don't know what I'm doing." Savannah raised her brows cheekily at her twin. "Or thereabouts. Oh, and I'm allowed to use my phone and it isn't stupid."

"You're so annoying."

Before Savannah could reply, the makeup artist stepped back and admired her handiwork in the mirror. "All done here. Go and get changed and then I'll finish your hair."

Ash looked in the mirror, she still couldn't get used to her hair being blonde. Sure, between the hair and the makeup she looked a little different, but she still saw herself looking back at her, not Frankie. Disappointed, she stood and headed for the door. "Are you coming?"

Savannah jumped to her feet and gave a little curtsy. "Whatever the movie star wants." She followed her twin out into the bright early morning sunshine. It was only a short walk before they were at Ash's trailer. It was gratifying to see Savannah's eyes go wide at her first glimpse of the luxurious accommodation they had provided for her. The Winnebago had quad sides that popped out to give extra space. The large main living area had been tastefully decorated with expensive looking rugs, cushions and throws in bright primary colors. On the kitchen bench were cutting edge appliances that Ash was too scared to even touch, let alone turn on. Personally, she'd thought the entertainment and gaming system was a nice touch, but had wondered when she was expected to have time to use it between being on set and learning lines.

"Oh my gosh, have you seen this?" Savannah held a tablet in her hand and began touching the screen. The blinds went up and the lights went out.

Ash quickly snatched it from her hands. "Stop that. What are you, a child?"

Savannah tilted her head at her blonde twin, dubiously eyeing her. "Don't even try to tell me you didn't do that as soon as you saw it."

"Well, maybe a little. But it's my trailer, so I'm allowed." She suddenly noticed a ginormous box that had been put in one corner. Seriously, it looked like it was big enough to hold a refrigerator. "Hmm, I wonder what this is?" Surprise, followed by confusion, made her do a double take. Abruptly, she held out a card to her sister. "It's for you."

Savannah looked at her suspiciously. "Why would this be for me?"

"I don't know, but your name's on it."

Her sister opened it and began to read the card, a delicate blush coloring her cheeks. She looked up, her eyes glowing warmly. "It's from Bryce."

Ash thought her sister looked quite pretty standing there all gooey-eyed. "Why is Bryce sending you stuff?"

"I don't know. It just says that he hopes I like them as much as he liked me in them." Obviously, it made sense to her and she began to open the box as Ash peered over her shoulder. Inside, the box was filled with neatly hanging clothes, which accounted for its bulky dimensions. Gently, Savannah pulled out a white dress. A single red rose had been pinned to it. "Oh," she whispered.

"What do you mean 'oh'?" Ash asked, watching her sister smell the rose and then hold the dress to her chest.

"Nothing. These are the clothes that I tried on for you the

other day. Or at least the same style. Bryce sent them to me as a gift."

Resentment flared up in Ash. Typical. It was her big day and Savannah was the one receiving gifts. She peered into the box. "Do you think I can have some of them?"

"No, these are mine. Maybe you can ask wardrobe if you can keep the ones you wear in the film."

"Knock, knock," Frankie's voice called from the door as she and the rest of the girls entered the trailer carrying a huge bouquet of flowers. The sight went a small way to mollifying Ash's earlier feelings of being forgotten. Frankie gave her a hug and handed them over. "How are you feeling, Ash? All ready?"

Ash chose to ignore Savannah's snort of derision, graciously accepting her gift. "A bit nervous, but I guess that's a good sign."

"Bloody heck, Ash. I can't get used to you as a blonde," Deb said. Ash's hand went self-consciously to touch her hair.

"I think she looks fabulous," Chloe said, giving her a hug too. "Maybe you should keep it afterwards."

"We don't want to take up too much of your time. I know you need to get changed and back to hair and makeup for touch-ups. I saw Martha on the prowl for you, too. We just wanted to wish you luck." Gabi smiled encouragingly. "Savannah, are you coming with us?"

Savannah gave her a quick hug. "You'll be amazing," she whispered.

Once the girls left, Ash put on the outfit that had been tagged for that morning's scene. It really wasn't too different from what she usually wore, but there was something about knowing it had been picked for Frankie that made her feel different. She was just finishing doing up her belt when Kirk popped his head in. "Hey, beautiful. I'm sorry I wasn't here earlier. Desiree had some things she needed to go over with me." *I bet,* Ash thought sourly. "How do you feel?"

"It's starting to hit me now. I'm not sure if I can do this," she admitted.

He picked up the trucker hat that had been sitting on the table and placed it on her head. "You will be fine. Just do it like we practiced. And I'll be there, okay?" He turned her to face the mirror. As she stared at her reflection, she saw Frankie staring back. She was Frankie.

CHAPTER 9

Spence Wittnall bit down on the end of the pen he held loosely in his hand, his eyes never leaving the screen in front of him. Ash sat beside Kirk, holding her breath, the anticipation reaching unbearable levels. Just as she thought she was about to pass out from lack of oxygen, the director pursed his lips and gave a sharp nod. "The camera loves them."

Beside her, she could feel Kirk relax. She'd been so caught up in her own tension that she hadn't even noticed he'd been sitting rigidly. "If you two can keep this up, you're Box Office gold." With that one sentence, all the doubts and angst of the previous week disappeared. Ash had never run on nervous energy so much in her life as she had since they began filming. The constant sensation of being on the wrong foot, never quite sure if what she was doing was what was being asked, had been draining.

Kirk kissed the top of her head, his approval and pride almost meaning as much to her as the directors. "I think we're only getting started."

Ash couldn't help but notice that Desiree looked like she'd

been sucking on a lemon. Surely the woman should be happy. Her client had just been told that he was doing a great job and the film had an excellent chance of being a hit. Mentally, she shrugged, too happy beside Kirk to waste any more time thinking about the stuck-up agent.

"Just wait till we get warmed up," she agreed, snuggling into her man.

SRA ANA GAVE a little disapproving sniff of the contents of the polystyrene cup. Tentatively, she poked at it with the little plastic spoon, the gelatinous soup resisting. How could the crew be expected to work hard with this in their belly? What about Kirk and Ash? they needed nutritious food, not whatever this was. A large man stood behind the bain-marie, watching on suspiciously.

"Is there anything else you want?" he asked.

"What is this called?" she asked politely.

"It's a vegan tofu soup."

"Thank you," Sra Ana said. This would not do. This would not do at all. She dropped her uneaten cup in the trash can and walked determinedly away.

SUZIE, the makeup artist, pulled a brush from the pouch at her waist and carefully selected blush from her palette before applying it vigorously to Ash's cheeks. "I heard you were doing an amazing job," she confided as she went about her work.

"Um, thank you. I'm just trying to not make a fool out of myself." Ash closed her mouth as Suzie started to line her lips.

"I heard the director say that he thinks you have real talent, that you could make a good career out of acting. He's claiming the credit for discovering you." Suzie exchanged the liner for another brush and began filling in Ash's lips with lipstick. "How hot is Kirk Cooper to work with? I mean, the man is gorgeous."

"It's been a great opportunity to work with Kirk." What more could Ash say? Kirk had changed her life and she couldn't imagine being on this adventure with anyone but him. He was everything she'd ever fantasized about in a man —strong, protective, caring. The hot packaging didn't half hurt either.

As if her mind had conjured him up, Kirk walked into the makeup trailer with his squinty-eyed smirk and gave her a kiss that made her toes curl. "Hello, beautiful. Ready?"

Ash smiled at him, warmth flowing with a delicious sensation from where her lips still tingled from his kiss. She reached out and grabbed his shirt, pulling him back down for another kiss. When they finally pulled apart, the look he sent her was pure male smugness, the woman in her responding.

Suzie gave a little tut. "Well, she was ready before you came along and messed her all up. Save it for the cameras, Romeo." She shooed him away.

Laughing, he complied. "I'll never get enough of her, cameras or not." Ash felt her face burn at the promise in his words.

THE BURLY MAN smiled down at the little Brazilian woman, gray streaking her hair. "Thank you, Sra Cabrera, I think I'll have another one of these. What do you call them?"

"Pao de queijo." Sra Ana smiled sweetly up at the man. "It is a family recipe. My children always loved them."

"I can see why," Suzie said. "I can already feel them going to my hips, but it's not going to stop me from grabbing another one."

"I don't know if I'll ever be able to pronounce it, but man, they are good," agreed someone else in the crowd that had formed around Sra Ana. She threw a victorious look over to the catering tent. The man standing at his station gave her a filthy look, one she answered with a sweetly innocent smile.

After her food had been gobbled up and she had begun packing up her hampers, the caterer angrily approached, frustration at her sabotage stamped on his ruddy face. "Look, I don't know who you are, but you can't be here handing out your food. If I see you around again, I'll have to call security."

"You can try, but they will not do anything if you do. This is private property, property that my adopted son and daughter own." She patted the furious man on the cheek. "I will keep bringing proper food for as long as you insist on serving what you are. I cannot let these poor people eat what you are making."

"Cut," bellowed Spence, rising from his chair. "That's a wrap, we'll move on to filming some of the riding scenes. Ash's double can fill in for that."

Ash could hear Savannah muttering under her breath. She couldn't understand why she was being such a pain about it all. Really, she should be thankful that she had the chance to be in a movie at all.

"You did great, beautiful."

Kirk joined Ash from where he'd been on the sidelines. Every scene she filmed, whether or not he was in it, he was there to support her. The first to bring her a drink or help her with lines or explain what the director wanted from her.

She didn't know if it was possible to love the guy more. He was complicated. Sometimes, he was her Kirk, the guy she had gotten to know on the ranch, and then he would say something to a crew member or Desiree would appear and he would morph into Kirk Cooper, the movie star. It made her feel like she loved a being that didn't fully exist.

"Kirk, I want you to attend the meeting with the stock contractor, Luciano, the animal wranglers, and stunt coordinators. I don't want to take any chances with the rodeo scene," Spence ordered.

"Right on it," Kirk said. He rubbed his hands up and down Ash's arms. "I'm not sure how long this will take. Do you want me to come over and run lines with you tonight, or are you okay?"

"I think I'm good. As much as I want to see you tonight, I'm exhausted. I think I'll just go to bed early."

He gave her a lingering kiss. "I'll give you a call when I finish to say goodnight then."

"I'll be waiting." Ash watched him go. They were setting up to shoot some rodeo scene several towns over. Kirk had been like an excited puppy ever since he had managed to talk Spence into letting him ride some of the bulls. And that was only after Luciano and Travis had vouched for him. A quick glance told her that Savannah had already left to get ready for her final scene of the day. It was nice to get a chance to relax, read her lines and have an early night. Sometimes having a twin came in handy.

Ash gave a sigh as she took off her boots. She wished they'd let her wear her own ones—at least they were broken in. Her costume boots had been given a worn appearance, but they hurt her feet just like brand new ones did. A knock sounded moments before her trailer door opened. Desiree was the last person she expected to enter.

"I wanted to come and check how you were managing."

She gave that false Hollywood smile, the one that was all gleaming white perfect teeth and no facial expression. "It can be overwhelming if you aren't really an actress."

Ash kept her expression neutral. She would rather die than let this woman know her little barbs got to her. "I guess I'm lucky. Kirk has made everything easier. He's helped me so much."

Desiree's eyes hardened, her face tightening so much that Ash wondered if she was in danger of chipping one of those perfect teeth. "Kirk will always do what's right for the film. He is Hollywood royalty, after all. He knows how things work, even if I suspect you don't."

"Would you like to just come out and say whatever it is you want to say, or should we continue beating around the bush?" Ash was tired of the pretense, the words always false and hollow.

"I've been in this business a long time and so has Kirk. My advice to you is don't lose your head. Enjoy your fling with Kirk."

"It's not a fling." Ash wanted to scream it at the top of her lungs. What she felt for Kirk, what he felt for her, wasn't some little fling. It was more than that, he made her feel like no man ever had. He made her feel loved.

"Oh dear, you have got it bad. But Kirk? He's only acting like you're a couple because it's good PR. Believe me, the public love it when the leads fall in love on set. But have you ever wondered why that only lasts for as long as it takes for the film to premiere?"

"You're wrong."

"We'll see. But do remember, I've known him a lot longer than you have. And I'll still know him long after he's forgotten your name."

CHAPTER 10

"Sra Cabrera this is the best coffee I've ever had." Martha cupped her fingers around the steaming drink in her hand. "I didn't even know it could taste this good."

Sra Ana nodded her head, accepting the compliment as her due. "We make it a little bit different in Brazil. The trick is to boil the sugar and water together before we add the coffee."

A flurry of customers left her thermoses empty, but her satisfaction full. A feeling that was further compounded when the caterer stomped over to her. She smiled sweetly at him. "I am all out now, but I can bring you a cup later?"

"You win," he ground out.

"I was not aware there was a competition."

He threw his hands up in the air in exasperated defeat. "Look, little lady, I know I can't beat you, but the fact remains that I was awarded the contract to cater for this film. Since you're going to be here whether I like it or not, you might as well start running the catering and come work for me."

Sra Ana's expression turned to pure business. It wasn't hard to see where her daughter got it from. She rubbed her hands together. "I will need to see what I have to work with. Show me your kitchen."

~

"It's all a bit bloody exciting, isn't it?" Deb craned her neck to take it all in. "I don't think I've ever been to a rodeo that isn't a rodeo."

"I think they did a good job setting it all up," Carlos said, his arm protectively around Megan as he held Edward on his other hip. "Where's Mitch?"

"He's hanging out with the animal wranglers. I'm not sure who's telling the biggest yarns."

Chloe had Teeny and Grace on either side of her on a bleacher in front of Deb. "I'm sure he'll find Travis at some point. I don't think the bulls have ever had so much fuss over their appearance before."

"I think you should be sitting down," Gabi ordered Frankie, pointing bossily to the seat. "Mae, make her listen."

Sra Ana looked up where she already sat beside Senhor Eduardo. "It is all very exciting, but maybe you should sit, Frankie. Your feet will start to ache."

"Should you even be here? A lady in your condition?" teased Deb. "I'd hate for you to pop early."

"Funny. All right, I'm bloody sitting. Is everyone happy now?" Frankie plonked down.

Ash let her friends' banter wash over her. Both her and Savannah had been allowed to be in the crowd as long as they were in disguise. A trucker hat pulled low was all it apparently took in movie land to become another person. She wondered how Kirk was feeling. She had swung by his trailer earlier, but he'd been focused on what the stunt coordinator and Luciano had been telling him. She'd tactfully left him to it.

A commotion began at the edge of the arena, the extras pointing and calling out. Ash could see Kirk making his way through the crowd, an arrogance she hadn't seen before as he strode forth. He walked as if a path had solely been laid for him, arrogantly oblivious to the unwashed masses that sought—nay, *fought*—to touch him. She was reminded of the desperation of trout battling against the stream. Ash was shaken by his demeanor. It was like he was the very embodiment of a celebrity and miles away from her Kirk. A voice crackled over the loudspeaker, calling for quiet.

"Kirk Cooper is on set. Take your places. Shooting is about to commence."

Ash settled back, the timber bleacher hard beneath her. She felt cold as she tried to shake off a feeling of unease, the feeling that the Kirk she knew might not exist. She'd thought the movie star was a character Kirk played, but what if she was wrong? What if Kirk was a role Kirk Cooper, the movie star, played instead?

KIRK LOOKED at the spittle fly through the air as the bull flicked his head, his horns smashing into the metal railing. Travis and Joao stood shoulder-to-shoulder, solid in their unspoken support. He tried to draw on their calm competence. Luciano stood slightly to one side, preparing himself for his own ride.

"Are you ready, my friend?" he asked, stretching, the leather of his chaps slapping against each other as he jumped and limbered up.

Kirk swallowed down his fear, it left a bitter taste in his mouth. He nodded, not trusting himself to speak. He tried not to notice Luciano give Joao a look, a look that spoke volumes.

"I, too, was afraid when it was time to get back on a bull after my accident. Travis can vouch for me. I walked away the first time. I was scared I would die, that I could no longer ride the bull. But I overcame it and became the Barretos champion." Joao lifted his belt to proudly show him the champion buckle that held pride of place.

"Dang it, man. Joao, don't tell him about dying." Travis rolled his eyes, "You bull riders might think that was a badge of honor, but city boy looks like he's going to be sick." He pointed to the restless bull in the chute. "This is one of my nicest bulls, Pansy."

Luciano laughed, his teeth gleaming under the bright lighting the riggers had set up. "I thought Teeny had stopped naming them after flowers."

"She did. But she said this one was special."

"Did you know that Travis's daughter rides all of his bulls?" Luciano asked.

Kirk stared at Travis in disbelief, his mouth dropping open. "Are you crazy, man? Why on earth would you let her do that?"

Travis shrugged. "Because she is safe. They're gentle as lambs with her." Kirk was beginning to feel a little wild.

The stunt coordinator approached them, talking into a walkie talkie. "Spence has changed the order. He wants Luciano to go first, and then you, Kirk. We will repeat that until we have the shots he wants." Kirk felt his knees go weak with relief that he had been granted a partial reprieve. Luciano smiled fiercely at the news, his eyes sparkling with anticipation. It was clear the Brazilian wasn't suffering any nerves.

Luciano handed his ropes to Travis and did a final check of his protective vest and clenched his gloved fist several times, the rosined leather creaking. "Ready?" he asked Travis.

At the other man's nod, he climbed the rail and began to lower himself on Pansy. The bull's skin twitched as Luciano's weight settled on him, his feet restlessly shifting. Kirk was fascinated as he watched Luciano wrapping the rope around his fist, opening and closing it until he was happy. Luciano pushed his Stetson down firmly on his head and, with his arm still resting on the rail, looked to the stunt coordinator.

"You will tell me when to go?"

The stunt coordinator passed the request on and waited, the affirmative response only seconds in coming. "We're good to go." An announcement echoed around the crowd of extras.

Luciano locked eyes on Kirk. "I will show you how it's done, and then you will fly, too." He gave a short, sharp nod of his head and the gate opened, the bull springing to life. Kirk gripped the rail tightly, unable to take his eyes from the raging battle in front of him. The bull plunged and twisted, desperate to rid himself of the man on his back. Dust clouded the arena, kicked up from the bovine's hooves.

Doubt began to assail Kirk from all sides again, this was meant to be a quiet bull. It felt like it was going on forever. The director had decided to go longer than the traditional eight seconds to get maximum footage for each ride. Finally, a bell sounded, letting Luciano know that he could dismount. Dismount sounded quite civilized for what was, in reality, the act of letting go and being launched into the air, hoping for the best. Well, that's what it looked like to Kirk. Luciano landed gracefully on his feet before beating a hasty retreat to the side of the arena as the bull was herded through a side gate. The Brazilian whooped and then pointed back to Kirk, as if to say, 'Your turn now, boy'.

"We're going to start with the shots of you getting on the

bull and then in the chute," Spence said, having made his way over for last minute directions to Kirk. "Once we have those, we will move you onto the bull Luciano just rode. That way, when we splice the footage of both rides together, it will give us continuity." Kirk nodded, absorbing the directions. "Let's get you on your mark and we'll start."

Kirk took his mark and began to settle into the character of Luciano. He waited for the call, rolling his head on his shoulders. "Action!"

A cameraman came in close, panning in as he zipped up his protective vest. His questing fingers found the crucifix that dangled from the shoulder strap. Muttering a prayer, he turned his head and kissed it. Flexing his gloved hand, he strode determinedly to the chute rail, the cameraman moving smoothly out of his way. In a fluid motion, he climbed the rail and stood, feet spread, one foot on a rail each side of the chute, suspended above the bull. He flicked his chaps out of the way and lowered himself onto the bovine's back. His stomach clenched as the animal moved beneath him before settling down. He turned his head and spat to one side, steadying his nerves. Grabbing the rope, he began to wrap it around his hand, hitting it with his other to secure the grip. Resting his arm on the rail as he had seen Luciano do earlier, he set his face and nodded.

"And cut. Now let's do that again," Spence called. Travis reached through and gave the bull a bucket of feed and scratched his head as Kirk was helped off.

Luciano made his way over to stand with Joao on the sidelines. "You will be an expert at getting on and off the bull before you ever need to worry about riding one."

"Maybe that is what we did wrong?" suggested Joao. "All I know is he is getting paid more than we ever did."

In reality, it didn't take half as long as Kirk would have

liked before they set up the scene for his actual ride. "Any last questions?" the stunt coordinator asked.

"I think I've got it. Hang on, look like I'm not scared, don't get killed." Kirk sent a side glance to Luciano and Joao, their mischievous grins making his seem suddenly boyish. "Is that about right?"

"We've got nothing left to teach you," agreed Luciano. "Do me proud."

Kirk went through the motions, settling himself on the bull. He could feel his heart beating, the blood pounding in his ears as he waited for his cue, the signal the gate would open and then there was nothing left that anyone could do but film what would happen next. The crowd of extras grew silent, waiting for direction to cheer. Somewhere out there was Ash. He hoped she was impressed. What a stupid thought! He was sitting on an animal that weighed nearly a ton and had the sole goal of trying to get him off his back anyway he could, and he was worried about whether Ash was going to be impressed or not.

Dimly, he heard "Action!" and the gate opened, Pansy springing into action. Nothing could prepare him for the raw power that rocketed underneath him. He struggled to keep his free hand out and away from his body. The bull's head disappeared in front of him, the force of the hindquarters causing his upper body to slump forward. He felt like he was strapped to an earthquake. He could only hang on and hope for the best. All he knew was that Luciano and Joao were insane to willingly choose to do this. He felt the point where his weight shifted too far to one side. Knowing he wouldn't be able to right himself again, he released his hold and let himself hit the dirt ungracefully.

"Cut!"

Kirk could feel the adrenaline course through him, his body trembling with it. He let out a loud whoop. Now he understood why Luciano had done it earlier, it was like an affirmation of life. He'd done it. He'd ridden a bull and survived to tell the tale. He felt invincible. From the crowd of extras, he saw Ash push her way through, her dyed-blonde hair escaping her trucker cap, as she sprinted across the sand to him. He missed her beautiful auburn hair.

"Are you impressed?" He wondered why it was so important to him what she thought.

"Kirk, I've been impressed since the moment I met you." She snuggled into his arms. If he'd thought he felt ten feet tall and invincible before, it was nothing compared to how she made him feel. "Kirk, you know what would impress me more?"

"What, beautiful?"

"If you'd kiss me."

There was no way in the world he was going to resist that command. Around them, Spence quietly gestured for the cameraman to start filming.

"Box Office gold," he muttered. "24-carat Box Office gold."

CHAPTER 11

*A*sh still couldn't believe that filming was almost over. It only seemed like a week ago that she'd been a nervous wreck, worried she was about to make a fool of herself and not knowing her gaffer from her sound assistant. Now, she could barely walk through the trailer village in the morning without being greeted every step of the way. She was going to miss the camaraderie that she had found on set. Sure, when it was all done, she would be back on the road with Savannah, hauling to rodeos. But she wasn't sure if that was going to feed her soul anymore. She might, she admitted in the depths of her heart, have been bitten by the acting bug. *Along with the love bug*, a little voice niggled.

She wasn't too sure how things were going to work out with Kirk. She was realistic enough to know that they had been in a little bubble—a bubble that was about to pop. Like Cinderella after the ball, she was going back to life on the ranch and he was going to return to the bright lights of Hollywood. Determinedly, she tried not to dwell on it. And if it worried her that Kirk never mentioned what would happen to them once filming was over, well, she pushed that thought away, not daring to think about it too closely.

Today, they were filming the final scene. It had taken her a while to get used to the fact that a movie wasn't necessarily shot in chronological order. One day, they could be shooting a scene from when Luciano and Frankie first met, and the next when he went to Barretos. But Spence had insisted that the final scene of their love story would be shot as the final scene of filming. He'd explained that he wanted to harness the emotions that would come with it being the end. That the actors would naturally be more overwrought and allow themselves to become excessively emotional.

Ash teared up every time she thought about the big will-you-marry-me world championship scene. She had seen footage of the actual event and, at the time, when she was a teenager, had thought it was the most romantic thing she'd ever seen. Now, to be playing Frankie seemed surreal. Ash sighed. There was no putting it off any longer. She opened her trailer door—showtime.

The camera panned in close and Kirk knelt on one knee. "Will you marry me, Querida?"

Ash felt the tears well up in her eyes. The way he looked at her, she felt like there was no one else for her in the world, heart filled to overflowing. "Yes, so much a yes." He stood with a whoop and swung her around in his arms.

"And cut. Reset the scene and we'll go from the top again." Ash sighed dejectedly at the call. She was exhausted. She hadn't realized just how emotionally taxing it would be to be proposed to again and again like some weird Groundhog Day. Martha's assistant appeared at her side and began to apply a lint roller to her clothes.

"How you hanging in there, kiddo?" asked Suzie as she retouched her makeup.

"Like this is never going to end, and then I feel bad because I don't want it to end."

"Welcome to movies. I feel the same way. Every time, I swear I'm going to get into editorials, but then another offer comes through and I can't resist the excitement of a new project. I'm off to Peru after this. I've just signed up for an action film."

Ash smiled her congratulations. She was going to miss the gossipy woman. She glanced over to where Desiree had sequestered Kirk. Now there was a woman she wasn't going to miss.

Suzie followed her gaze. "You'd think she'd let it go already."

"What do you mean?"

"I guess you wouldn't know, but then I guess I just kinda figured someone would have mentioned it to you by now." Suzie secured her brushes back in the pouch at her waist.

"Are you planning on putting me out of my misery at some point?"

"I guess." Suzie smiled cheekily at her, the diamond set in her canine tooth winking in the lights. "Well, it's just that, for one hot minute, Desiree and Kirk had a thing and I'm not even sure it lasted long enough to be called a thing."

Ash stared. She could feel her face wrinkling unflatteringly, not sure what to make of the information. It certainly made sense of the other woman's hostility. What she wanted to know was what it meant for her future—a future she wanted to share with Kirk.

ASH SWIRLED her drink as she looked around the wrap party.

She was emotionally drained. Sure, she'd been expecting some sadness. But the intense sorrow and loss that hit her when Spence had called, "Cut, and that's a wrap, ladies and gentlemen"—that had hit her from out of nowhere. Ash wondered how these people did it, movie after movie. Then she remembered that they knew they would all work together again at some point. For her, she would never be able to repeat this experience or share it with the people that she had. She would never get to play a character falling in love while she fell in love herself again. She was going back to her plain old life on the ranch. To be fair, it wasn't the end of the world. But now, she wanted more. She wanted bright lights and fast cars driven by handsome actors—or one handsome actor in particular, to be specific.

Beside her, Kirk was engaged in conversation with one of the gaffs who had come up to say goodbye. He definitely acted like a star around them and the crew loved him. What surprised her the most was watching, one by one or in little groups, people coming up to Sra Ana, crying and hugging her as if they were saying a last goodbye to a beloved family member. Senhor Eduardo was even standing guard over a bundle of gifts that she had received as the sobbing cast made declarations of never forgetting her and promises of visits. Ash's interest was piqued when the burly caterer approached. This time, Sra Ana was the one to give him a gift. He opened it to reveal what appeared to be a book and smiled, perhaps the first expression of joy she'd ever seen cross his face. Ash managed to capture a glimpse of the tome and it looked to be handwritten. He held his arms wide and enveloped the little Brazilian lady before discreetly wiping a tear from his eye as he walked away.

"Beautiful, I'm going to get another drink, would you like one?" Kirk leaned in close, his expensive aftershave filling her nostrils with its delicious fragrance.

She smiled up at his gorgeous face, that half smirk she'd grown so used to staring at. A sickening feeling threatened to choke her when she thought about not seeing it every day. "I'd love another champagne."

"Whatever the lady wishes is my command." Ash couldn't help admiring the view as he headed to the bar.

"I always find wrap parties tend to be a bit dull. Everyone's behavior is so repetitive. The lower crew members get drunk and make fools of themselves and the power players come for a drink to be polite and then make their excuses to leave." Desiree sidled up beside Ash, making the hairs stand up on the back of her neck. "But you're probably enjoying yourself. It's the first one for you, isn't it? It seems like your kind of scene. I guess I'm just a bit blasé about it all. I've been to so many."

"I'm enjoying myself and so is Kirk." Ash gave her a level look, daring Desiree to contradict her.

"Kirk deserves to let loose a little. He starts another film almost straightaway. They expect him on set in Peru in two weeks."

Ash silently congratulated herself for not giving any sign to this venomous woman that it was news to her. Maybe she was a better actress than she gave herself credit for. "Ah, here's my newly minted star," Spence announced dramatically as he approached with Kirk. Ash thought Desiree's smile was so brittle it was in danger of shattering. "I would happily work with you again. It will be a privilege to watch you grow as a thespian. But no matter who you work with, I predict you will achieve great things."

Ash blushed under his praise, blinking away tears that sprung to her eyes at his approval. She had grown and learned so much from the director and she would always have a special place in her heart for this man who had shown faith and buckets of patience to her. She hugged him fiercely.

"Spence, I'll never forget this experience. Thank you for everything."

Desiree placed her hand a little too familiarly for Ash's liking on Kirk's arm. She didn't miss the possessive look that was sent her way either. "Kirk, darling there are some things I want to talk to you about."

Kirk looked irritated at her presumptive tone. Desiree, not reading the sign, looked smugly at Ash when he laid his hand on where hers rested on his arm. A look that quickly disappeared into barely concealed fury when he firmly removed it. "Not tonight, Desiree. Anything you have to say can wait till the morning. Right now, all I want to do is drive fast and be with my baby." He held his hand out to Ash. "Ready, beautiful?"

"Always, Kirk." She couldn't resist sending her own smug smile back at her fuming nemesis. "Always."

"I REMEMBER the first time you drove fast with me in your flash city sports car." She laughed at the memory, trying to ignore the thought that it would soon be some other girl. She was painfully aware that he hadn't made any promises to her about what would happen after filming ended. Ash didn't want to believe Desiree, but wasn't it the sort of thing you read in the media all the time? Maybe she was naïve and being used. She peered in the shadowy light, trying to believe that Kirk was different.

"I have a film I need to start in a couple of weeks in Peru," Kirk said non-committedly.

"Yeah, I heard something about that. Not going to lie, it hurt a bit to hear it from someone else." Ash thought she was going to choke on the bitterness in her voice.

"I think I can guess who told you, but you know what,

Ash? You've never had any trouble voicing your opinion or questions before. All you had to do was ask."

There was something in how he said it that made Ash's spine stiffen. "Maybe I figured if you wanted me to know, you would tell me." She stared straight ahead, not willing to let him see how much she was hurting. "It's not like you didn't change or anything."

"What do you mean change? I've never treated you any different from the moment I met you. Or is that the problem? You didn't like me when I was just Kirk." The edge in his voice cut her to the core.

"That's not true and you know it," shouted Ash furiously. "But you did change. You are different now. As soon as filming started, you morphed into this other character. You became a movie star."

"I'm still me. But I told you before, that's not what people want to see. They want Kirk Cooper and, if I want to continue being successful and getting work, then that's what I've got to keep giving them." Ash felt like she'd been slapped hearing his cynical assessment. It was something she expected from Desiree, not Kirk. "Look, I don't want to argue. What I was trying to do was ask if you would come with me—to Peru."

"Why?" her voice was barely a whisper.

"What do you mean 'why'?" The truck sped along, gaining momentum. "It's not a hard question. Do you want to come to Peru with me or not?"

"I want to know why you want me to come." A terrible certainty settled over Ash, like a fog in a hollow on a cold winter's morning. She could feel the tendrils of ice snake around her heart. Desiree was right. There was no her and Kirk, it was all PR, just something for the media to write about. Heartbroken, she looked at him. He refused to even glance at her, staring straight ahead, his jaw set. "Why, Kirk?"

"If you think I'm going to beg you to come, Ash, then you're mistaken. I'm not that man."

Ash wanted to scream at him, to make him understand that she didn't want him to beg. But she needed to hear him say why, to tell her that he wanted her there. She desperately needed to know he felt like she did and the mere thought of being separated caused him physical pain, that he loved her. A surprised oath didn't even have time to register before the world spun madly out of control and then nothing.

KIRK DIDN'T THINK he would ever forgive himself for the previous night. He had let his anger get the better of him when he should have been focused on the road. All he had been thinking about was why Ash wouldn't let it go. Why was she pushing him for a reason? Didn't she know that he cared about her? Why did she need to hear the words? Or was it that she was like all the rest? He still remembered how stupid he'd been with his first love. His dad had tried to warn him, but the old man had always had a knack for ruining things for him. Michelle had been everything his young man's heart had wanted at the tender age of twenty-one. A childlike face hid a jaded heart, one that had set her sights on landing the son of the great Mason Cooper. It had taken her a full ten minutes after his declaration to go running to the papers, telling the world that Kirk Cooper was in love. It took her another ten minutes after that to run straight into his father's bed. Turns out landing Mason Cooper was better than his son.

But Ash wasn't Michelle, and he had been too busy stubbornly resisting Ash's attempts to get him to open his heart that he almost didn't see the cattle on the road until it was too late. He was so very lucky he hadn't killed her. Kirk's soul went cold at the thought. He had spent a sleepless night after Travis had arrived to collect his niece, insisting on driving both of them to the hospital to get checked out. Ash hadn't spoken a single word to him the whole time.

He scrubbed at his face with his hands. Today, he was going to make everything better. He was going to tell her how he felt and if he had to beg, well, that's what he was going to do to get the woman he loved to come with him.

As Kirk approached the barn, he could hear the girl's voices inside. Smiling, he stopped to listen to their chatter, waiting to hear Ash's voice.

"I almost had a heart attack when I found out you were in a crash," Chloe said.

"You and me both," agreed Savannah. "How's Kirk this morning?"

"I don't know, and I don't really expect to hear from him." Kirk's heart dropped like a stone weight at Ash's cold words.

"How hard did you bump your head last night? Of course you're going to hear from him again." Savannah's voice again.

"Look, Kirk was just a fling. It was never anything serious. It's what happens on movies and, when filming finishes, well, you guys can figure out the rest."

Kirk couldn't believe he'd let himself be played for a fool. She was just like the rest. What hurt the most was to him was that she hadn't been like them—she'd been special. Not wanting to hear another word, he climbed back into his car. Without looking back, he sped away back to the bright lights of LA.

CHAPTER 12

Surrounded as she was by her own miasma of gloom, Ash nonetheless felt that she wasn't alone. Gabi wandered around making comments that she had so much free time on her hands since the Hollywood circus had left. Sure, building had recommenced on the training facilities at Luciano and Frankie's ranch, but it wasn't the same. Even Sra Ana seemed a bit glum. It was obvious she had liked the excitement of having lots of people to mother. She was making up for it now that Frankie was finding being pregnant difficult. The growing twins inside her had made her belly huge and rather ungainly. Sra Ana now switched all her frustrated mothering to the beleaguered mother-to-be.

Ash wasn't sure where Frankie was. Or Gabi, for that matter. Chloe and Savannah were finishing up the last of the horses for the day and, since there was only two, Ash had been told to find something else to do. Feeling out of sorts, she had drifted around the barn until she had heard bright laughter on the breeze. Following the sound, she had tracked it down to its source under the live oak tree.

Sprawled out on a large multicolored rug in the shade

was Senhor Eduardo playing with Grace and Edward as Sra Ana watched on, talking to Megan. "Is this where everyone went?"

Ash flopped down, uninvited, on the rug, rolling onto her back and looking up into the vast canopy above her. The intricate pattern of branches and leaves silhouetted against the vast infinite blue of the sky. Ash found herself tracing the interplay of the light against dark with her eyes. She sighed, feeling adrift and lost.

"I do not mind all the peace and quiet as well," Senhor Eduardo said, mistaking her sigh for contentment. He wiped some dribble from Edward's chin. Ash marveled that he could have a look of such deep fulfillment cleaning bodily fluids from another small human being. "In fact, I am looking forward to no excitement for a while. Sra Ana is even letting me eat everything she makes, not like before when I had to smell all my favorite dishes being cooked, my mouth drool-ing, and then she'd slap my hand away and say it is not for me, it is for her crew."

"I miss my crew," Sra Ana said dejectedly. "I hope they are eating properly."

Ash focused on the pattern above her again, trying not to think about what was now in the past—the crew, the film, Kirk.

"Does anyone know where Luciano is?" Deb gasped out, having run the entire distance from the barn.

Senhor Eduardo raised himself up on his elbow to look at Deb in astonishment. "I think maybe he is with Joao or perhaps Carlos."

"Mom, maybe you should have walked instead of run. You sound all puffy, like that old dog at the feed store," Grace said with the humility that only the young can produce so guilelessly. Ash secretly agreed with the comparison.

"Not now, Gracie. Why is no one answering their phones?

I can't get a bloody hold of anyone." Deb began to pace frantically, her audience watching her, open-mouthed, their heads following her movements back and forth. "I have no idea where Gabi is. For once in her life, she isn't answering her bloody phone either. I've got Mitch heading over to Joao's and Gabi's to try and find them."

Megan slapped her forehead gently. "Sorry, I just remembered. I think Carlos said he and Luciano might be heading out to look at some heifers. I'm sure they'll get back to you." She smiled down at her son, her face softening in a way that always surprised Ash, considering how tough she usually was.

"You don't understand. Frankie thinks she's in labor." Pandemonium followed her announcement.

Senhor Eduardo leapt to his feet. "Why did you not say so earlier?" He looked at Sra Ana. "We must go to Frankie. She will need us, my love."

Sra Ana nodded, her eyes shadowed with concern, her mouth pursed as if to hold the worry in. "It's too early, but the doctor did say to Frankie that sometimes twins do not want to wait."

"We came early," Ash agreed, hoping it would help calm everyone down.

"Megan, Ash, can you please stay with the kids? I'm going with the Cabrera's to be with Frankie. If anyone sees Luciano or Gabi or *anyone*, tell them to call me." Deb's long strides easily overtook the older Brazilian couple as they rushed to their truck.

Ash decided she would have to take back her earlier feeling of boring and quiet on the ranch now. Instead, it was like that phrase Frankie was always saying—never a dull moment.

~

"AND THEN DEB SAID, just when they thought Luciano would miss the whole thing, he came tearing into the maternity ward, like he had the hounds of hell on his heels. The midwives took one look at his crazy expression and wanted to kick him out." Chloe laughed as she told the twins. Ash could imagine the Brazilian yelling for his Querida and making a scene, demanding to know where she was.

"But did he make it?" Savannah leaned forward on her elbows, chin buried in her hands.

"Yes, which I think is lucky. I'm not sure Frankie would've forgiven him if he hadn't been there for the birth of his children. I swear, it's so bloody typical of those two. They never do anything by halves." Chloe's phone beeped and she looked down at it. Ash could tell by the gooey smile on her face that it had to be something about the babies. "Aww, guys, have a look." She turned the screen around for the twins to see. "This little cutie here is Harper"—she pointed to the slightly smaller of the squishy red-faced infants—"and this is her big brother by three minutes, I'm told, Luciano Junior."

Ash looked at the photo. Luciano had a baby in each arm, his face split in two by the biggest smile she had ever seen him wear. And that was really saying something. Luciano was always flashing that grin of his around. Frankie looked tired. No, that wasn't the right word. She looked exhausted, but somehow like she was glowing from within. There was a contented smile on her lips, one that Ash had never seen, like she'd somehow achieved her greatest dream, finally reaching some sort of great pinnacle in her life. She did have to give the couple credit. The babies looked adorable, both having inherited their father's dark hair.

"A boy and a girl. Sra Ana must be over the moon," Savannah said.

"Apparently she can't decide who to fuss over and keeps going between them. Deb says it's so cute. Gracie has already met them. I'm going to go tomorrow to visit them with Travis and Teeny, if you guys want to come with me."

Savannah looked questioningly at Ash. "Do you want to? We need to get her a present first." She worried her bottom lip with her teeth. "Do you think we'll have time to get one before we visit?"

"I don't think we will, but how about we find something online and tell her it's coming? I mean, no one was expecting her to have the babies so soon. We didn't even have a baby shower for her."

Chloe laughed. "Babies not waiting to arrive when they're meant to is becoming a bit of an Affinity Ranch tradition. I'm sure Frankie won't mind."

"Well if you think it will be okay, we'd love to come," Ash said, surprising herself that she was looking forward to meeting the babies. She wasn't, by nature, particularly maternal. But then again, most girls her age weren't except for Chloe, but she was pretty sure that girl had been born clucky. "Did they end up finding out where Gabi and Joao were?"

Chloe's eyes opened wide with secret delight. "I can't believe I forgot to tell you about that. Yep, they found them. Turns out they were already at the hospital."

"Why? Was Joao having a checkup?" Ash asked.

Her friend's eyes sparkled, her secret begging to be told. "Well, that's the best bit. It wasn't Joao that was having the appointment, it was Gabi. She was getting scans to confirm she's pregnant and she is!"

CHAPTER 13

"I don't think we should split the present for Frankie and the baby 50/50," Savannah said, bringing her laptop over to show some gift ideas to Ash. "It's clear she likes you more."

"That's true, I am her favorite." Ash modestly blew on her nails and pretended to buff them on the leg of her jeans. "I mean, she did select me to play her in a movie about her life after all, but we're still splitting the present 50/50."

"The casting director selected you to play her and it was Gabi that suggested you." Savannah folded her arms tightly over her chest as her foot tapped in annoyance. "Anyway, you got paid more than me when we did that film. How about 70/30?"

"Of course I got paid more than you. I had lines and a little thing called, oh that's right, the lead actress!" Ash felt a stab of loss. It was the first time all day she had allowed herself to think about the movie or the real reason for the heavy weight in the pit of her stomach—Kirk. She mentally brushed it off. No way was she giving that jerk the satisfaction of making her feel blue. "I don't think so. How is 70/30 fair?"

"60/40?"

"No."

"55/45?"

"Deal." Ash peered over Savannah's shoulder to look at the images she had on the screen. A delicate musical carousel caught her eye. "That's pretty."

"I was just thinking that. Happy to buy that one?" Savannah looked up when Ash took a little too long to answer. Ash could feel her sister staring at her, knowing she wasn't blind. But how could she tell her sister how unhappy she was? Even now, Ash could feel herself drifting off into a melancholy sadness, a lethargy that wanted to hold her close. She was lost, aimlessly adrift, and couldn't find a reason to return to her usual self. "Do you want to talk about it?"

"Huh? Talk about what?" Ash flopped down on the couch and turned the TV on.

Savannah gently took the remote out of her sister's hand and turned it off. "Even if I wasn't your twin, I'm not stupid. Why don't you call him?"

Ash stiffened before giving a deliberate shake of her head, her mouth forming an angry 'O' as she let out a forceful breath. "And why would I do that?"

"Because you obviously miss him."

"Miss him? He used me, Savannah. He made me feel like somehow, when he was with me, I let him be the real him and I was the only one that had ever made him feel that way. He must think I'm such an idiot for falling for it. I bet him and Desiree laughed about it, too."

"I don't think they did. Ash"—Savannah sat down on the couch beside her—"I saw how he was with you and I don't think he was pretending."

A rage so pure it was terrifying rushed through her. She

felt a primal urge to hit out, to take something in her hands and destroy it. Ash picked up an earlier discarded coffee mug beside the couch and threw it against the wall. Savannah jumped out of the way of the hurtled missile, knowing she wasn't the target, but still not trusting her sister's aim. The mug exploded satisfyingly into shards.

"Don't you get it?" she yelled. "That's what he does. He pretends. He's an actor." Ash's bottom lip began to tremble. Furiously, she scrubbed the tears from her eyes, daring Savannah to say anything. "He made me believe he cared and then he left. He didn't even say goodbye."

Savannah wrapped her arms around her sobbing sister. "Then you're right. He's a jerk and he doesn't deserve you. Maybe the best thing we can do is get back on the road and start competing again. You know, get back to what we do best?"

Ash sniffed. How could she ever explain to her twin that she wasn't even sure what that was anymore?

IRRITATION WELLED UP INSIDE ASH. If Savannah looked at her one more time like she was some poor sympathy case, she really was going to throw something again. She crossed her eyes and stuck out her tongue at her sister. Chloe, oblivious to the interplay between her friends, cooed over the twins held snuggly in Luciano's arms. Ash was beginning to wonder if the man ever put them down.

"Have they told you how much longer you need to stay?" Chloe asked.

"About a week, just to make sure Harper catches up a little bit more to her brother." Frankie beamed over at her babies. Or maybe it was her husband. Ash couldn't be sure.

"I hear congratulations are in order," Savannah said,

helping herself to some chocolates on Frankie's bedside table.

"Why didn't you say anything?" Chloe asked, her pretty blue eyes finally shifting from the babies.

Gabi cleared her throat, looking uncomfortable and then oddly sad. "Um, I guess it's no good hiding it now. Joao and I've been trying for a while and we did manage to get pregnant, but we lost the baby at seven weeks."

There was a stoic acceptance to her words that made Ash want to weep. "Why didn't you say anything?" Frankie cried. "We should have been there for you. We would have been there if we'd known."

Gabi squeezed her friend's hand, smiling sadly at her. "There were so many exciting things happening. I didn't want to steal anyone's spotlight by making a big pregnancy announcement. We were planning on waiting, and then a few weeks later, I had a miscarriage." Ash thought back to when they had shot the rodeo scene, to how sad Gabi had seemed.

"I still wished you'd told me or one of us. You and Joao shouldn't have had to go through something like that by yourselves. It doesn't matter how busy or exciting things are, we're family. Did Sra Ana at least know?"

"I did tell her and Papai, but I asked them to keep it quiet. That's why, this time, we wanted to really make sure before we told everyone. Surprise." Gabi threw her hands up in the air.

Ash couldn't fathom how Gabi could function after losing a pregnancy. She might not have any experience herself, but she knew enough to know that there was something very special about knowing that life, no matter how early, was growing inside you. Unconsciously, she patted her own belly. Here she was moping around after a good-for-nothing movie star like she had lost everything. In front of her was a woman that had every right to crawl into bed and pretend the world didn't exist. Instead, Gabi chose to function, albeit still bereaved, but determinedly moving forward.

Ash resolutely set her jaw and hardened her heart. Goodbye, Kirk Cooper.

CHAPTER 14

Country music played between the announcer's voice booming over the loudspeakers, updating the crowd on times and scores, sending them into a frenzy of hooting and hollering. Ash swallowed, her mouth dry from the dust in her throat as she sat. The leather of the saddle creaked, her horse shifting his weight from one hind leg to the other.

Absentmindedly, she swished an errant fly away from her face, watching the familiar scene of livestock and folk milling around behind the chutes and warmup area. This used to her world, one that she lived and breathed for. Now she felt like an outsider to her own tribe.

Glumly, she wondered if it was too late to fake an illness to withdraw from the event. Knowing Savannah would be horrified at her thoughts, she looked guiltily around, spying her twin with Miranda. Ash gave a shiver of distaste at Savannah's new friend. There was something that just didn't vibe right about her. To be fair, she had never given Ash a direct reason not to like her. It was just a little look or subtle way she said something that made her Spidey senses go all tingly.

Ash scrunched up her face as she thought about the few times she had tried to say something to Savannah. Okay, maybe she could have worded it better, but she hadn't expected her sister to jump to her new acquaintance's defense so fiercely when she'd called her weird. And who was Savannah to call her judgmental, anyway? Her, judgmental? It wasn't her fault there were so many strange people in the world.

Heaving another sigh, she gathered up her reins and clucked to Jazz—might as well get it over with—and loped her horse over to join her sister. Ash made a sour face at Miranda's shrill laugh as she approached. Honestly, what did Savannah see in this woman? She fixed a stiff smile on her lips, momentarily reminded of what her mom used to tell them as kids when they would pull faces. Mom used to say, "Be careful. the wind might change, and you'll be stuck like that."

Ash wondered if she wanted to be stuck like this. Not her face, but here, doing this, for the rest of her life. Thinking about Kirk still hurt a whole lot more than she wanted to admit, but if she took him out of the scenario, making that movie had been one of the most exhilarating experiences of her life—and she was a crazy cowgirl, after all. Spence had been encouraging in his appraisal of her talent. Maybe she could call him and talk over some options, maybe get an agent and see what happens. The only thing she knew was that her heart wasn't in barrel racing anymore.

"I DIDN'T KNOW Bryce was going to be here." Ash set a beer down in front of Savannah, glad that, for the time being, they had managed to shake Miranda. She figured it wouldn't be long before the annoying woman found them. Determinedly, she shook all thoughts of her from her mind. Why ruin the moment?

Savannah craned her head about, trying to spot Bryce in the crowd. "I can't see him." She turned disappointed eyes back to her beer. Ash privately thought Savannah needed to get her crush for the cowboy businessman under control. Sure, they flirted, but Bryce had had ample opportunity to ask her out and he hadn't. If that didn't tell a girl something, she wasn't sure what did. "He's over at the bar."

Nervously, Savannah smoothed down her hair. "How do I look? Is he still there?"

Ash leaned over to one side to see past her twin. "Nope, he's not there anymore." She settled back in her chair and grabbed her beer. "But if it makes you feel better, I can see where he is."

"Really?" Savannah placed her hands on the table and spun around, finding herself unexpectedly facing Bryce's chest.

"Darling, my eyes are up here." Bryce's voice was warm with amusement and bourbon. "And you haven't even bought me a drink yet."

Savannah, mortified, turned narrowed eyes accusingly to her sister. Ash simply smiled innocently and shrugged. "Evening, Bryce. How did you enjoy the rodeo?"

Bryce's hand rested on the back of Savannah's chair. "I've never been to a rodeo I didn't enjoy. May I join you lovely ladies?"

"I'd love it. I mean, we'd like that." Ash couldn't quite contain the snort that her sister's words caused. Savannah's color was high as Bryce, ever the gentleman, put on an appearance of having not heard as he retrieved a chair from the nearby table and seated himself.

"What brings you here?" Ash asked. It seemed too small

an event for Bryce to be visiting one of his sponsored team members or have sponsored the rodeo.

"I wanted to check in and see some of the improvements Joao has implemented with the Black Angus Sports Medical Team." He sipped his drink. "And then I saw two of my favorite people sitting here and, well, how could I resist?"

"Hey, Savannah." Ash cringed at Miranda's high-pitched voice. She knew it had been too good to think she would stay away for the rest of the night and let the girls enjoy a few drinks after finishing their events. It didn't escape her notice that only Savannah had been greeted. Judging from Bryce's raised eyebrow, it hadn't slipped past him either.

"Hi, Miranda. I don't think you've met our friend, Bryce." Savannah placed her hand familiarly on his arm. "Bryce, this is Miranda. Miranda, this is Bryce."

"Ma'am." Bryce touched his fingers to the brim of his hat and nodded, but remained seated, not offering a hand to her in greeting. The cut from the ever-polite cowboy was telling. Ash knew there was a reason she'd always liked him.

Miranda offered Bryce a plastic smile. Ash was fascinated by the undercurrents swirling around the table. Miranda was a strange one, that was for sure, but if she thought she could play at intimidating Bryce, she was in for one heck of a shock. Ash fervently prayed she would be around to see her get her comeuppance.

"Want to come to the bar and get some drinks with me?" Miranda asked Savannah, playing with her freshly dyed red hair, a shade eerily similar to the twins'.

"Ash just got me one, thanks." Savannah focused her attention on Bryce. "Did you like what you saw?"

"I like what I see very much. I noticed you're wearing some of the clothes I sent you."

"Oh." Savannah smoothed down the sleeve of her top, caught off guard. "Yes, I am. Did you get my thank you message? It was such a generous gift, but that's not what I meant. I meant the changes Joao has made."

"I sure did. But I offered him the job because I knew he would make a success of it. I try to surround myself with people that take an opportunity and run with it."

Miranda tugged insistently on Savannah's sleeve, drawing her attention away from Bryce. Ash felt herself ever so slightly lean forward, insanely curious what was going to happen next. "Gosh, can you hear it?" Miranda pointed to the dance floor. "They're playing your favorite song."

Bryce offered his hand to Savannah. "Would the lady care to dance?"

Savannah went a rather fetching shade of pink, her green eyes sparkling with excitement. "I would love to, Bryce."

Ash smiled at the peevish expression on Miranda's face. "I'd say that's one for Bryce, zero for you." Suddenly enjoying herself immensely, she took a swig of beer and watched her sister dance. Tonight was definitely improving for the better and, to top it all off, she happened to not even think about what's-his-name once.

CHAPTER 15

The rack of dresses, all neatly hanging in their protective bags, stood in the center of Ash's room. A veritable who's who of designer labels, a vision that should set a girl's heart a flutter in the way only expensive clothing could.

Savannah stormed in, popping the bubble of anticipation that had been building inside Ash as she prepared to free the first creation from its plastic cocoon. "Never text me 'help' in all caps again when you discover cellulite. I thought you were dying!"

"I am dying … dying from old age." Like a switch, Ash's mood changed, bordering on hysterical at the thought of her dimpling dilemma. "Do you want to see it?" She sobbed, showing her the offensive skin.

Savannah's bottom lip stuck out in sympathy as she gathered Ash close. "It's going to be all right. It's not that bad."

"We're getting old. We're going to look like Mom."

"Probably, but at least I don't have cellulite." Savannah took a closer look at the rack behind Ash. "Are these the dresses they sent over for the red carpet?"

"Yeah, I was just about to start trying them on."

"Well, what's stopping you?"

Muttering to herself, Ash pulled the first one off the rack and unzipped it. First impressions were not kind. It looked like the contents of the Muppets' off-cast bin had thrown up onto burlap. "What on earth is this?"

Savannah wrinkled her nose. "Maybe it will look better on?" she said doubtfully. It didn't.

The next offering was what could only be loosely defined as a gown in the stupendously boring color of beige and took the twins five minutes to get Ash encased in it. The main fabric appeared to have been made by sticking old doilies together, which could have been a nice effect in theory. The sleeves were ruffled, puffy concoctions roughly the size of bowling balls and, to cap the outfit off, it featured a bizarre feathered hood.

"Oh my." Savannah giggled, taking in the overall visual. "This is quite a look."

"A look? I look ridiculous is what you mean." Ash marched over to the rack and opened each of the remaining offerings, anger mounting as each outdid the one before it.

"Wow, they're all really gross." Savannah held her hand aghast to her mouth. "Who did you annoy for them to do this to you?" A little giggle escaped from behind her hand.

Ash gave a sweeping gesture with her arm, taking in the haute couture disaster before her. "Who do you think? Desiree." She bared her teeth as she said the loathed name.

"Oh." Savannah pressed her lips together. Ash wasn't sure if it was to hold in her laughter or because she felt sorry for her. She was leaning toward the former. "Well, that makes sense. There's no way she would want you to look good."

Ash folded her arms. "And here I was thinking she was a professional."

"Well, according to my source, she's hoping for round two with Kirk, if you know what I mean."

Ash froze, not sure how she should feel. Surely not an overwhelming urge to punch the absent Desiree in her trouble-making mouth. "How do you know this?"

"You remember Suzie? The makeup artist?"

Ash rolled her eyes. "Of course I remember Suzie. I only saw her, like, every day for two months."

"Well, she's the makeup artist on Kirk's current film. She says it's starting to get a bit embarrassing how Desiree's acting," Savannah said with evident relish. "It's the scandal of the set how obvious she is."

There was a sick feeling in Ash's stomach at the thought of the two of them together. "I bet Kirk's just eating up the attention."

"Apparently no. Suzie says he's like a recluse and won't come out of his trailer unless he absolutely has to."

Ash digested the information. Her legs felt weak with relief—kinda like the time she thought running a marathon at school would be a good idea. Her heart fluttered hopefully as she sunk down on the bed. "Why would he do that?"

Savannah looked at her sister as if it was obvious. "Because he doesn't want her. I think maybe he liked you a whole lot more than just a fling."

"Then why didn't he say goodbye?" Darn it, she'd promise herself she wouldn't cry over Kirk Cooper again. Resolutely, she blinked back the tears.

Savannah pulled her sister in close and leaned her cheek against Ash's head. "I don't know, and you obviously don't either. So why don't you just call him or email or whatever—carrier pigeon, for all I care—and ask him?"

It sounded so simple when it was said like that. Just pick up the phone and talk to him, hear his voice, and perhaps have a chance of it all falling back to how it was. And then her heart snapped shut against the warm fuzzy fantasy before it could even fully form in her mind, all the hurt crashing back in. She was not going to be another Desiree. Someone that he had a bit of fun with and discarded, who couldn't take the hint that it was over. "Yeah, well, he has my number, too. He knows where I am. And I'll be darned if I'm going to chase Kirk Cooper."

MAYBE SHE SHOULD CALL HIM, give him a chance to explain himself. Mentally, she gave a little shake. No, she was going to stop thinking about him. Ash plastered a smile on her face, determined to be present for this joyous occasion. Frankie had finally been allowed to bring the twins home. Everywhere, it seemed, she was surrounded by happy couples, children and babies. She got some perverse pleasure that Savannah was still as single as her.

A delivery man arrived, causing a commotion as he walked into the party carrying a large box he could barely see over. "Is there a Harper and Luciano Jnr here?" he asked.

Gabi laughed. "Yes. Do you need them to sign for this?"

"Yes, ma'am."

She pointed, still giggling to where Luciano and Frankie stood cradling their babies. "Before you get too excited, Harper and Luciano Jnr are the babies."

"Oh. I think it would be all right if you signed then, ma'am." With a quick flourish, she complied and sent the relieved man on his way.

"Frankie, Luciano, delivery," Gabi sang out.

Everyone clustered in close, curious to see what treasure the box contained. Frankie pulled a card from an envelope taped to the side of the parcel. "It's from Bryce, with his apologies that he couldn't make it." She looked around thoughtfully. "I'm beginning to think that he doesn't like babies." Everyone laughed at her comment before urging her to open the present. One after another, Frankie pulled out infant versions of outfits both her and Luciano had worn at their various wins over the years.

"I didn't think he would actually do it," exclaimed Savannah, turning pink when all eyes focused on her.

"You knew he was going to do this?" Frankie asked, marveling over another tiny outfit she held up.

"Well, he mentioned something when I saw him last."

"I'm amazed he got to say anything with all the gushing you did around him." Ash teasingly batted her eyelashes at her sister.

"You guys seem to be spending a lot of time together," Gabi observed, sending suggestive looks to the older women in the group.

"Oh, it's not like that. We haven't been out or anything. I don't even have his number. I just think he's a really nice guy." Savannah trailed off as she became aware that she might have revealed too much.

"And you were the one that gave me the advice to just call a guy," murmured Ash, enjoying seeing her sister on the receiving end of her own advice.

"Ash," her sister said after a moment.

"Yeah?"

"So, which dress did you pick to wear for the premiere?"

Ash stared hard at Savannah. "Shut up."

Savannah picked a tiny pair of jeans out of the box. "These really are cute, don't y'all think?"

CHAPTER 16

*A*fter Ash had returned the hideous dresses with a note to not bother and she would find her own outfit for the red carpet, she had assumed that was the last she would hear about it. She had half-heartedly made an attempt to start the search, but she just couldn't muster the enthusiasm to throw herself into it. It wasn't helped by the fact that she had no idea where to start with finding something suitable for a Hollywood premiere on her limited ranch hand budget. *Tomorrow,* she promised herself. *Tomorrow, I will go to the mall and find something.*

"Ash, I just signed for a parcel for you," called Savannah, carrying in a large flat box. "What on earth have you ordered from Amazon now?"

"Nothing," denied Ash, whilst at the same time wondering if they sold fancy LA dresses on there. She made a mental note to check later, just in case.

"Well, open it up then." Savannah shoved the box at her sister and sat down, impatiently waiting for the contents to be revealed.

"And they say I'm the pushy twin."

Ash swept back some of her recently redyed auburn hair from her face. It had felt good to no longer be blonde, like she was herself again instead of playing at being someone else. Someone else, like an actress in love with her famous co-star. Irritated at the unbidden thought, she ripped open the unoffending box more aggressively than it warranted, tearing the cardboard asunder to reveal a plastic garment bag inside.

"Geeze, Desiree doesn't give up. I wonder what monstrosity she's sent me this time."

Savannah almost ripped the bag as she pulled it excitedly from Ash's hands and laid it out on the couch, beginning to unzip it. Slowly, the plastic fell away as she gently lifted it from its plastic cocoon, revealing black silk embroidered with intricate jet beading.

Ash held her breath reverently as the full creation emerged, Savannah holding the hanger high with one hand and the other flaring out the full skirts. The black silk and beading covered the entire dress except for a two-inch band at the top of the bodice that was silver silk with a silver and gold beaded pattern. "It's beautiful," she breathed.

"That's not all. There's another bag in the box as well." Savannah laid the dress over the couch and ferreted about the torn parcel to retrieve the other items. A white faux fur wrap that was so luxurious all Ash wanted to do was snuggle her cheek against its soft surface. "Ash, there's a note in here that says jewelry—earrings, necklace and cuff, to be precise— will be delivered to your hotel room on the day."

"It looks like something out of a magazine."

"Well, put it on. I'm dying to see what it looks like on you."

Ash gathered the dress up in her arms, beaming with excitement at her twin. "You just want to know what you'd look like in it, too."

"That too, now hurry up."

Her fingers trembled as she slipped into the dreamlike creation, the fabric surprisingly heavy. She wiggled it into place and then added the wrap. "How do I look?"

It was gratifying to see Savannah's mouth open into a perfect 'O', her eyes wide and shimmering. "Oh, Ash, you look like a princess. Quick, have a look in the mirror."

The colors were elegant against her skin and hair tone. The bodice formfitting to her waist and then flared into graceful folds of shimmering, swirling skirt. It was classic golden Hollywood, as far from the trashy dresses she had been sent as humanly possible. "I wonder what made Desiree have a change in heart?"

"Um, well, I'm pretty sure she hates you as much as usual. I might have said something to Suzie." Savannah guiltily pulled a face. "And she might have said something to Kirk."

"Oh, Savannah, you didn't."

"And he might have called in some favors and apparently he picked the dress you're wearing himself."

Ash turned back toward the mirror, her emotions matching the swirling beadwork on her dress. Why would he go to all the trouble to find her such a gorgeous gown? It felt strangely intimate to stand in an outfit Kirk had selected, that he'd touched and thought of her wearing it. She shivered, the silk whispering deliciously against her skin.

"He did a better job than Desiree." Ash smugly looked over at her sister. "I can't wait to see her face when she sees me in this." *And that goes double for when she finds out Kirk gave it to me,* she silently added.

~

THE CABRERA HOUSEHOLD was fit to overflowing with women and gowns trying to make final selections before they began to pack and get ready for the LA premiere. Carlos and Mitch had volunteered to stay back at the ranch to look after everything and Chloe had offered to travel to LA to babysit the kids at the hotel while everyone else attended the red-carpet premiere and afterparty. Personally, Ash thought she was crazy to miss out on it all and try and keep two babies, a toddler, and a six-year-old under control. Honestly, there were times she just didn't understand the girl.

"You should see Ash's dress," Savannah was telling Chloe. "It's like something you see at the Oscars."

"I wish you had brought it over to show us, but I understand why you're keeping it as a surprise. So much more dramatic this way." Gabi, stunning in a pale bronze dress, nodded her approval at Ash, causing her to smile happily back at her, lapping it up.

"Frankie, have you got your bloody dress on yet or not?" Deb called, smoothing down her own royal blue gown. "We need to get a picture of us all standing together so we know if we clash or not."

"You know they're only going to be taking pictures of the actors and maybe Frankie and Luciano, right?" Megan asked, her gown a light sky blue.

"And what happens if they want one of all of us and we clash? Then what, Megan? Do you want to be on the front cover of a magazine looking like a packet of skittles?"

"Okay, guys, I'm almost ready. I just need someone to zip me up." Frankie shuffled out, holding her red dress up awkwardly. Gabi quickly went to her aid and Frankie stood to her full height and gave a twirl. Ash thought she looked stunning. It still amazed her that she had been picked to portray this incredibly beautiful woman on screen.

Suddenly, Harper—or was it Junior?—started to cry. "Oh no, oh no, oh no." Frankie frantically began to wave her hands about. Ash looked around in alarm, not quite sure what all the fuss was about. When she looked back at Frankie, two large wet spots had appeared on the front of her dress.

Sra Ana reached into her pockets and pulled out some tissues and hurried over to Frankie. Ash took a moment to appreciate that the Brazilian woman had found an evening dress that came complete with pockets. The woman was a treasure.

Frankie started to cry as Sra Ana blotted at the fabric of her dress. "I can't leave my twins for the night. No offense, Chloe, I know you will take good care of them, but I've never been away from them."

"None taken," Chloe said from where she rocked the now content twin.

"And what if this happens on the red carpet? I would die from embarrassment," wailed Frankie.

Deb grabbed a handful of tissues and stuffed them down the front of Frankie's dress. "We'll just make sure you have lots of padding in there and you won't have to worry about a thing. Plus, if you start crying during the film, you can just reach in and pull out a tissue."

"The padding makes your boobs look amazing," Megan eyed her appreciatively. "Luciano won't know where to look."

Deb patted the last tissue in place. "Oh, I'm sure Luciano will know exactly where to look."

CHAPTER 17

*A*sh flopped, exhausted, on the bed. It was official. LA was crazy. Everyone had arrived that morning ready for the premiere the following night. With a day free, it had been unanimously decided to sightsee, and what sights they had seen. First cab off the rank had been Venice Beach. Sure, Ash had seen pictures before of the famous boardwalk with its palm trees, but they hadn't done it justice. She hadn't known where to look first. It was loud and colorful. At some stage, some skateboarders had zoomed past her and then a muscle-bound trio had sauntered by and winked at them. She'd given all the cash on her to the various buskers. Gracie had to be coaxed from the snake charmer, and Megan and Deb had gotten into a heated conversation with doomsdayers.

From there, the group had headed to Rodeo Drive and it was there that, for the first time, Ash felt like she was out of place. Slender perfect women teetered past on impossibly high heels and short dresses, white teeth flashing from tanned faces. They reminded her of flamingos and, although there were other tourists there, only the Affinity Ranch group were on the receiving end of the stares and titters. Ash had looked down at her cowboy boots and jeans, embarrassed that she looked so out of place. Luciano and Joao hadn't noticed as they had spent the entire time taking turns at having their pictures taken with the luxury sports cars parked.

Over a leisurely lunch at a hideously expensive restaurant, Frankie had suggested they finish the day seeing the Hollywood Walk of Fame. After all, they were movie folk now, she'd said earnestly. As jaded as Ash was beginning to feel from the day's outing, even she had gotten a thrill at seeing the stars of the Hollywood greats, icons her mom had made her watch the films of growing up. She wondered how it would feel to one day have her star here amongst the legends. Lost in her thoughts, she'd silently trailed behind the excited group until her eyes had found Mason Cooper's star. She wondered if he knew just how much his presence had overshadowed his son's entire life, or if he even cared.

Laying now on the hotel bed, her thoughts drifted to the son once again. She still hadn't heard from him, and if it hadn't been for the beautiful gown he'd sent her—her eyes sought out where it hung safely in the wardrobe—well, she would've assumed he hadn't thought about her at all. When she reflected on him just leaving and not saying goodbye, the complete radio silence ever since, well, the humiliation stung, but the hurt was what made her heart ache. Tomorrow, in front of everyone, she was going to have to bury those emotions so deep in her soul that no one would be able to see what it cost her.

Savannah walked from the bathroom, her toothbrush in hand. "My feet hurt so much I don't think I'm going to be able to walk in the new shoes I'm wearing with my dress. How are yours?"

Ash wiggled her toes experimentally. "Not too bad. Hey,

Savannah, do you think maybe we could order some popcorn from room service and sit up and watch a movie, like how we did when we were little with Mom?"

"Sure, I'm still bummed that Dad and Mom couldn't make it with Grandma having her surgery on the same day. I mean, what were the odds of that happening?" Savannah's words were muffled by the toothbrush in her mouth. "Are you feeling nervous about tomorrow?"

"Yeah, and a lot of other things." Ash rolled onto her stomach and hugged a pillow tight. "I want to enjoy every minute of this. It's my first ever premiere and it might be my last one, too. But no matter what, tomorrow will be special, and I get to share it with you and the others."

"I feel like there's a but in there." Savannah headed back to the bathroom. "Hang on a second, I'm just going to rinse my mouth and then I'm all ears." Ash could hear gurgling noises and then the tap turning off as she stared around at the luxurious room that had been appointed to them. She had never stayed anywhere as fancy as this. "How do you feel about seeing Kirk again?"

Trust her twin to confront the white elephant in the room head on. She sorted through all the tumbling, confusing emotions the mere mention of Kirk always caused. "I'm dreading it, but there's this sense of anticipation. Kinda like there's unfinished business and, one way or the other, it will be dealt with tomorrow. One thing I do know is I'm going to look so hot when he does see me, he's going to have a major case of regret."

"I don't know if I'm scared for Kirk or not." Savannah picked up the room service menu.

"Me neither." Ash giggled, suddenly feeling light-hearted at having worked her thoughts into a manageable place in her head. "Now, do they have chocolate brownies on there?"

"Are you allowed to eat? I'm sure I read that all of the

Hollywood actresses go on a fast for twenty-four hours before a red-carpet event." Savannah ducked as a pillow came sailing through the air, aimed at her head. "Hey, I'm just looking out for you."

"If you're looking out for me, you'll order that brownie."

"Geeze, you do one little movie and now you're a diva."

Ash grabbed the remote and began to flick through the channels to find a movie. Kirk better hold on to his hat. This diva was about to make him sit up and take notice.

CHAPTER 18

The chair was beginning to feel uncomfortably hard. Ash shifted her weight to try and ease her discomfort as she focused intently on what the interviewer was asking her. She had been awake since shockingly early and she promised herself she was going to have words with whoever thought it would be a good idea to have someone fire questions at her while she nervously prepared. Thank goodness the hair and makeup artist they had sent to her was Suzie.

"I understand that you had not had professional training before this film, and I've heard from various sources that Spence Wittnall thinks you are a rising talent. Do you see a future in film after this?" The journalist stared at her expectantly, waiting for a newsworthy reply.

"Spence is an amazing director and to hear him say such nice things about me is flattering to say the least." Ash paused, not entirely sure what to say next. "I enjoyed the experience a great deal and, if another amazing script came my way, I would definitely pursue it." Phew, she breathed out a sigh of relief that she had managed to say something without saying anything substantial.

"Finally, I hear there was major chemistry on set between you and Kirk Cooper, who plays the male lead. In fact, a little birdie told me that some of that spilled over into real life. Would you like to comment?"

Suzie casually began to apply product to Ash's hair, somehow getting distracted and accidently spraying some into the journalist's face, causing his eyes to water as he coughed and spluttered. "Oops, can I get you a glass of water?" she asked solicitously.

Savannah appeared at the man's elbow. "Unfortunately, I believe that's all the time that was allocated to you. Ash appreciates you coming by and looks forward to reading your article. Now, if you would like to come with me, I believe Ash needs to finish getting herself ready for the premiere." The journalist seemed shell-shocked and put up very little resistance as her twin escorted him from the room.

Suzie chuckled. "I hope you don't mind, but I thought you might not want to answer that question."

Ash reached over and clasped Suzie's hand where it rested lightly on her shoulder. "It was like you read my mind."

"I think it's time to get you into your dress and then I'll finish your hair and do any final touchups. Can I just say how amazing your hair looks? I'm so glad they got it back so close to its natural color."

Ash touched her hair gently. "So am I. It's true, blondes have more fun, but redheads get into more trouble. Now, let's get this dress on."

Suzie was just applying a final coat of lipstick when a knock sounded on the door. "I'll just go see who it is," Savannah said, rising from her chair where she had been sitting, careful not to get her own dress crushed.

From the corner of her eye, Ash saw a man hand over a small package and a whispered exchange take place. Her curiosity piqued, she waited for her sister's return. "What did he want?"

"To give you this." She handed over a velvet box. Ash stared at it uncertainly before snapping it open. Inside, on a satin lining, lay a diamond necklace with matching earrings and cuff. "He also instructed me that he would be escorting you this evening as the diamonds are worth a million dollars."

Ash was almost too scared to touch them, almost. Gently, she tilted the case to allow the diamonds to capture the light. "They're gorgeous," she breathed. "But why would they lend such valuable jewels to me? I'm nobody."

"But Kirk Cooper is somebody and he requested them for you." Savannah gave a shrug. "Or at least, that's what the guy just told me."

Ash's stomach flip flopped at the news. There he was again, making sure she had what she needed for her—*their*—big night. Why was he pulling strings behind the scenes to make sure everything was perfect, but she still hadn't seen or heard from him? Surely, he was back in town by now.

"Here, let me put them on you." Suzie gently took them from her hands and began to secure them around her neck before moving to her ears and finally, her wrist. Critically she looked her over. "I've done all I can." She stepped away to give her access to the full-length mirror.

Ash looked at herself in wonderment. Her hair had been swept back into an artfully arranged bun, her locks sleek and glossy against her head. Smokey eye makeup made her eyes such a vivid green that it looked like she was wearing color contacts. "I look like another person."

"You look like a movie star," Savannah corrected her. She draped the white faux fur wrap around her shoulders and stood behind her, looking at her sister reflected back at her from the mirror. "You look beautiful. Now, let's go and show him what he's been missing."

~

"I WISH we'd been able to all come in the same limo," Ash said to Savannah as their car pulled up. Nerves jangled up her spine, making her feel the urge to bolt as she spied the red carpet and paparazzi lined up behind velvet ropes, intent on getting the money shot. Behind them, she could see reporters and then, further along still, fans.

Savannah clutched her hand. "It looks crazy out there. Are you ready for this?"

"No."

Adrenaline spiked through her system, her heart palpitating, and her chest tingling. Before she could even take a deep breath to calm her nerves, a valet opened the door and held a hand out for her. She gave an anxious grimace to Savannah before accepting it and, clasping the fur wrap with her other hand, stepped out into the bright lights.

Momentarily, she was blinded by the flashing lights of the media's cameras. Feeling disorientated, she took a step backwards and felt Savannah's hand on her bum pushing her forward. "Seriously, Ash, you need to let me get out of this car," she muttered from behind her.

Putting on her best smile, one that she had been practicing in the mirror all week, Ash raised her chin and began to saunter down the red carpet. Ahead, she could see some members of the cast and Spence already being interviewed, little huddles of media around them. She smiled when she saw Frankie looking radiant in her red gown and Luciano in his cowboy finery talking to a reporter. It really was happening. She was walking the red carpet of her very own movie premiere. Striving for a casual sweeping glance, she tried to see if she could find Kirk and was disappointed when she failed to locate him. "Ash, Ash Decker, over here," the paparazzi called, trying to get her attention to pose for them.

She reached deep down into her soul and pulled up all the confidence she had ever possessed and sashayed over. "Showtime."

~

ASH HAD NEVER GIVEN enough credit to how tired your hand got when signing autographs, not to mention how much her cheeks hurt from smiling for all the photos with fans. "Everyone needs to start making their way into the cinema please," a security guard said, beginning to usher people along.

Kirk had still not made an appearance on the red carpet. Ash was trying to do her best not to take it as a personal insult that he didn't want to walk it with her. Her thoughts were so tangled up. He'd sent her the gown and jewelry, but then wasn't here to see her in it. She leaned in for a final picture with a fan and hoped all they saw when they looked at the image later was an excitedly glowing actress.

Over the dispersing crowd, she could see a limousine pull to an abrupt stop and, like a scene from a movie, Kirk stepped out, buttoning his evening jacket up. The sight of him slammed into her like a sledgehammer, her heart beating faster as the crowd faded into the background. His head turned, scanning the crowd, looking for someone. Ash realized, her heart singing, that he was looking for her. Their eyes locked and it was like the last few months disappeared. Ash knew then that she was just as much in love with him as she had always been but had not been willing to admit it. He gave her that familiar squinted smirk and she was falling all over again. In his eyes, she could see a question, one she was now ready to answer.

The security guard cleared his throat. "Miss Decker, I'm gonna need you to head inside for me."

"In a moment. I just need to wait for—" Her heart dropped like a stone as Desiree stepped out from the car and said something to Kirk. He nodded and walked over to where the media were calling out for him. Desiree sent Ash a smug look, one that quite clearly said, 'He will always do what I tell him'. Ash allowed the guard to take her elbow and lead her inside, dejected that she had lost the moment and the chance to speak to Kirk. She cast one final glance over her shoulder to see him watching her go, his expression unfathomable.

CHAPTER 19

*A*sh found her place beside Spence and noted that there was a free seat on the other side of the director, one she assumed was for Kirk. Up on the screen, interviews from the cast and crew that had been recorded during filming played. It was fun seeing what people had thought and it made her feel nostalgic. Kirk took his seat beside Spence just as the interview Ash and he had given together started. She didn't know where to look as they flirted with each other. It was obvious they'd shared more than just on-screen chemistry.

Spence leaned over to her. "Now, it's our turn to get up." She followed his lead and, with the rest of the cast and crew, made her way to the front of the cinema. The director patiently waited for the thunderous applause to quieten down. "I'm really excited to be here tonight. This story leapt off the pages as soon as I read it and I knew I wanted to tell the story of Luciano and Frankie Navarro." Joao whooped from the crowd. "I would like to thank the cast and crew for all their efforts in making this film as good as it is." More applause from the audience. "Special mention has to go to my leads, Kirk Cooper and Ash Decker. Would either of you like to say a few words?" Ash shook her head but, to her surprise, Kirk commandingly held his hand out for the microphone.

"Working on this film was an incredible life-changing experience for me." Ash stared at him, her heart clenching painfully. "The opportunity to work with a director of the caliber of Spence Wittnall was a dream come true, and I will always cherish the time we spent together as a cast and crew. I would also like to thank Luciano and Frankie and the rest of the Affinity Ranch family for their generosity in helping turn this city boy into a cowboy. Words will never convey what it meant to me." His eyes lingered on Ash for a poignant moment before he handed the mic back to Spence.

"Well, without further ado, I'm proud to introduce our movie, A Bull Rider's Paradise." As the audience applauded, everyone made their way back to their seats for the screening to begin.

Ash decided it was a special kind of torture to be separated by a single seat from the man she loved and not be able to talk to him privately, to tell him how she felt and what a fool she had been to wait so long. As the movie unfolded, she swore she could see them falling in love right there on the big screen. She looked at his shadowy profile and wondered if he saw the same thing, if his heart called out as hers did.

ASH DISCREETLY DABBED a tear from her eye as the credits rolled. Behind her, she could hear her friends praising the film, but for now, she was content to remain in her seat. It had been an emotional rollercoaster and she was drained. The lights flickered on quicker than she would have liked, but still she remained seated whilst everyone else stood.

"Darling, you were amazing," she heard Desiree praise Kirk. Ash stuck out her tongue and pretended to gag.

"Oh my gosh, Ash, you were great." Frankie gave her a hug as the rest of the group came forward to congratulate her. "I wasn't sure how it would feel to watch someone else tell Luc and my story, but you nailed it perfectly."

Megan, Deb and Savannah clustered around. "I thought the horse-riding scenes were done expertly." Savannah buffed her nails.

"That's because you did it." Deb gave the other woman a nudge with her shoulder. "And you'll never bloody guess who just happened to be sitting next to Savannah."

Ash looked at her twin with interest, noting the blush. "Someone needs to have words with Bryce. If he keeps giving Savannah all this attention, people might start talking."

Savannah lifted her chin defiantly. "Well, let them talk. Because there's nothing to talk about." She trailed off, sounding a little disappointed at her situation.

"Are we going to stand around here all night or head over to the afterparty?" Megan grumbled.

"I'm amazed you can bloody well fit any more in. You should've seen how much popcorn she's eaten once she found out it was bloody free," Deb said.

"Leave her alone," Gabi instructed. "Seriously, I thought we left the kids at home tonight. But are we going or not?"

Ash finally found her emotional equilibrium and stood up. "I hear it's going to be one heck of a party and I, for one, wouldn't miss it for the world."

CHAPTER 20

*A*sh led the way into the party, swiping a cocktail off a passing waiter and downing it as she scoped out the action. She was just about to comment on the décor when her empty glass was taken from her hand and she was unceremoniously placed over someone's shoulder. She gave a little shriek as she desperately tried to tug the top of her dress to get herself covered, hoping she didn't spill out in front of everyone. Her friends grew smaller and smaller as they stood watching her get carried away. Looking down from the broad shoulders she dangled from, she spied a firm bottom that looked suspiciously familiar.

"Kirk Cooper, you put me down this instant!"

"Not until you've heard what I have to say." He grabbed hold of a door handle and yanked it open before closing it with a thud once they had stepped inside. From her upside-down position, it looked to be some sort of coat room. Slowly, he lowered her, keeping their bodies disturbingly close together until, at last, Ash's feet touched solid ground. Even then, he held her firmly, her hands having nowhere to rest but on his chest. Through his evening coat, she could feel the hard muscles beneath. She moved her hand until it rested over his heart, the organ beating rapidly under her palm.

"Do you want to explain yourself?"

His eyes narrowed as he stared down at her, she wasn't sure if he was frustrated or trying to intimidate her. "Do you have any idea how hard it was to stay away from you?"

Her treacherous heart leapt at his words, her pulse racing with hope. "Apparently not that hard at all since you left without saying goodbye and I never heard another word from you till now."

"I did come to say goodbye." His words were so soft she almost missed them.

"Excuse me?"

"I did come to say goodbye, but then I found out you and I were only a fling." He glared at her, challenging her to deny it.

She futilely tried to push against his chest, squirming to get some space between them. Ash didn't want to have this conversation anymore. It felt like she was standing on quicksand and she didn't know what to say. "In the beginning, I thought you wanted to have something real with me, but then it changed as soon as Hollywood turned up on our doorstep. I believed you when you told me it was how people expected you to act, but then Desiree explained it to me." Ash tried again to shove him away, her anger mounting. "And darn, I can't believe I was so naïve to think you actually cared about me."

Kirk's arms were firm against her, not letting her escape as his features hardened. "What, exactly, did Desiree have to say?"

"That it was all an act for publicity. That it's just how it works in the movie industry." Ash almost choked on her bitterness.

"She lied." Kirk's hazel eyes drilled into her, not giving her an inch to escape that probing look. "Maybe some actors do that kind of thing, but I'm not one of them. What we had was real or, at least, it was for me."

Ash's breath bottled up inside of her, hope fighting its way through the confusion that clouded her thoughts. "But you changed so much. By the end of filming, all I wanted was the Kirk I first met, the one that could just be himself. That's the man I fell in love with."

He became so still Ash wasn't even sure if he still breathed. She knew she wasn't. "I thought I was just a fling? That's what you told your sister."

"I never told her that," she denied hotly.

"Yes, you did." The fire in his eyes matched her own. "The morning I came to say goodbye, you told your sister that it wasn't serious between us. It hurt to hear the woman I was about to tell I loved her and beg her to come with me just write us off as nothing special, just some fun."

Ash tried to make sense of what he was saying, horror dawning as she thought back to that morning and how her stupid pride and wounded ego had made her act like she didn't care. "I didn't mean it. I was hurting. You have to understand that I was confused by how you were acting and then what Desiree said—it's no excuse, but I didn't know what to think." She blinked as his statement fully penetrated her brain. "Did you say you were going to tell me you loved me?"

"Yes."

"Do you still?" She swallowed. "I mean, do you still love me?"

"I spent the whole time I was away filming hating you and loving you in equal parts," he admitted. "But I never could get the hate to make the love go away."

Ash's bottom lip trembled. It felt like her insides were shattering at his words. "What did I do?"

"What did we both do?" He gently cupped her face. "Tell me right now, do you love me?"

"Yes." She blinked back some tears, painfully exposed beneath his gaze. "You have me all tied up in knots, but so help me, I love you."

"I love you, too. I can't believe the pain you put me through. But I guess we're both guilty of that. I swear I'll always be myself around you, but—" She saw raw vulnerability reflected back at her. "No one has ever wanted just me."

She gripped his face fiercely between her hands. "That's what I want. That's all I've ever wanted and all I ever will want."

He clasped the back of one of her hands and turned it to kiss the palm gently. "Then you've got it. But you need to remember that sometimes I need to be the movie star too."

"I love Kirk, but I can put up with Mr Movie Star once in a while. If he becomes too much of a pain, I'll just have to take him down a peg or two."

He chuckled. "It sure isn't going to be boring, is it?"

"Well, it might start getting boring if you don't kiss me soon."

"I've always been good at taking directions." As his lips claimed hers, outside, the fireworks display lit up the sky, the party goers cheering wildly. Inside, a cowgirl simply smiled at her movie star, luxuriating in their love.

EPILOGUE

The gossamer curtains fluttered in the briny sea air that floated up from the canal below. Ash could just glimpse the blue of the water, crisscrossed with the whitewash of passing boats. Never in her wildest dreams did she imagine she would be in such a grand palazzo. Momentarily distracted from her reading, she surveyed the opulence that surrounded her. The duck blue of the silk wallpaper was very pretty, she supposed, but it only served as a foil to the magnificent white, cream and gold frescos on the ceiling. The porter had told her that they were original to the building and almost seven hundred years old.

She settled back into the plush pillows of the bed and resumed her reading. Venice wasn't too bad a place to live while Kirk filmed his latest movie. Today had been one of his rare days off and they had spent the morning exploring before returning, content to be in each other's company in their suite of rooms. A giggle escaped her as she read.

"What are you reading, beautiful?" Kirk asked as he walked in, having finished a conference call with the director.

She showed him the script. "It's for an action movie."

Kirk laughed and picked up a script that was laying on top of his bag. It was the exact same one Ash was reading. She giggled at the coincidence.

He looked her up and down. "I can see you as a kick-butt action star."

She tried to do her best superhero pose on the bed. "That reminds me, I need to call Savannah and see how she did at her last rodeo." She set the script aside and wiggled to the side of the bed, resting her chin in her hands. "Did I tell you what happened while we were getting reacquainted at the premiere?"

"No, but I wouldn't mind getting reacquainted now."

Ash fended him off, laughing. "Apparently everyone started looking for us, but Savannah had seen us go into that room and she stood guard outside. Every time someone tried to look inside, she told them she had already checked and sent them on their way." She giggled at the thought. "She said she really enjoyed it, especially giving Desiree the runaround, but she did start feeling bad for the security guard that thought he had let me run off with a million dollars' worth of diamonds. Speaking of which, I wonder if Desiree has managed to get herself some more clients now that she has lost her number one star." She pulled a feigned pouting face.

Kirk jumped on the bed and rolled Ash over. "I don't know. And I don't care."

Ash blinked innocently up at him. "Oh, what do you care about?"

"Let me show you."

As he kissed her, Ash couldn't help but feel it was good to be a cowgirl loved by her movie star. Very good indeed.

THE END

As an Indie Author, reviews help me get my books noticed. If you enjoyed reading Ash's story as much as I did writing it, please leave a review. It will make all the difference to me.

If you loved, *A Cowgirl's Movie Star,* sign up for my newsletter to get exclusive bonus bits.

Now, turn the page as the Affinity Stud Ranch story reaches its finale with Savannah's story…

A COWGIRL'S BILLIONAIRE -
SNEAK PEEK

The popcorn crunched, the saltiness mixing pleasantly with the bourbon Bryce washed it down with. He sat, a sole island, alone in his lavish media room, intently staring at the screen that dominated the opposite wall. The movie panned in to show the side profile of the actress on screen, her blonde hair flying behind her as she urged her horse onwards.

"I don't know why everyone has trouble telling them apart. Savannah has always been the more beautiful of the two."

He took another sip from his bourbon, his phone finding its way unbidden into his hand. It would be so easy to call Gabi and get Savannah's number, to hear her sweet voice on the line. Bryce's hand trembled as he battled with himself. No, he couldn't do that to her, no matter how much he wanted it. With a muttered curse, he threw the popcorn, the puffy kernels exploding against the unoffending wall. Drunkenly, he put his face in his hands and sobbed.

. . .

Savannah's story, A *Cowgirl's Billionaire*, is available for purchase on Amazon or free on Kindle Unlimited

ACKNOWLEDGMENTS

A debt of gratitude to my editor Rebekah Groves for her patience with me.

Another big thanks to Megan from Designed with Grace for her cover design. Who knew it was so hard to get pictures of hot cowboys that were wearing shirts.

To my amazing beta readers and street team, you guys rock and I couldn't do it without you

A cowgirl adrift. A broken billionaire cowboy. Can he free himself from the past to be the man she needs now?

Christmas Standalone Books

Boots and Mistletoe

ABOUT THE AUTHOR

Edith MacKenzie or Eddie Mac to her friends is an author of sweet and wholesome contemporary cowboy romance. They say in literary circles to write what you know, and Eddie has certainly taken that to heart. Before embarking on a writing career, she trained horses professionally and brings that wealth of knowledge to her writing.

Now a mum to a boy and girl, as well as wife, she delights with her tales of strong cowgirls and their adventures in finding love. When not weaving the love stories of her characters, she enjoys hanging out with her family and animals, as well as reading, fishing and camping.

Just remember—once a cowgirl, always a cowgirl.

facebook.com/EddieMacAuthor
amazon.com/Edith-MacKenzie
bookbub.com/profile/edith-mackenzie

GLOSSARY OF AUSSIE SLANG

Now everyone knows that cobbers from the Land Down Under speak the Queen's English, but if you don't know to Tracky Daks from your Servo, I've put together a quick little cheat sheet.

A few stubbies short of a six pack - Crazy

Ankle Bitter - Small child

Arvo - Afternoon

Blind - Intoxicated

Bloody - Very. Used to extenuate a point

Bloody oath - Yes or its true

Bludger - Someone who is lazy

Buggered - Exhausted

Cark it - Die

Choccy Bikkie - Chocolate cookie

Clucky - Feeling maternal

Crook - Feeling sick

Daks - Trousers e.g. Tracky Daks are tracksuit pants

Dog's breakfast - Messy (does not relate to food), a bit of a shambles

Dry as a dead dingo's doing - Exceptionally dry

Flat out like a lizard drinking' - Not doing very much at all

Grog - Alcohol

Hit the frog and toad - Hit the road, get going

Man's not a camel - A man gets thirsty and would indeed like the beverage you are offering him

Mate - Friend or conversely could be someone you barely know

Nay, Yeah - Yes

Pull the wool over someone's eyes - To trick or mislead someone

Reckon - For sure

Ripsnorter - Can also be interchanged with beaut, bonza. Someone doing something exceptionally good

Servo - Petrol Station

Six one way, half a dozen the other - Undecided

Sparrow Fart - Before the crack of dawn. Very, very early in the morning

Stone the flamin' crow - An utterance of surprise of annoyance

Struth - God's truth. Used to express surprise or dismay

She'll be right - Everything is going to okay

Tell 'em they're dreaming - Is never in a million years going to happen

Tighter than a fish's bum - Said person is very frugal with their money

To blow smoke up someone's bum - To give praise that might make the other person cocky or overly confident

Up yourself - Stuck up

Ute - Pickup Truck

Whoop whoop - Middle of nowhere

Wrap ya laughing gear 'round that - Eat this

Yarn - To talk or tell tall tales

Yeah, nay - No

You bloody ripper - Very good, a job well done